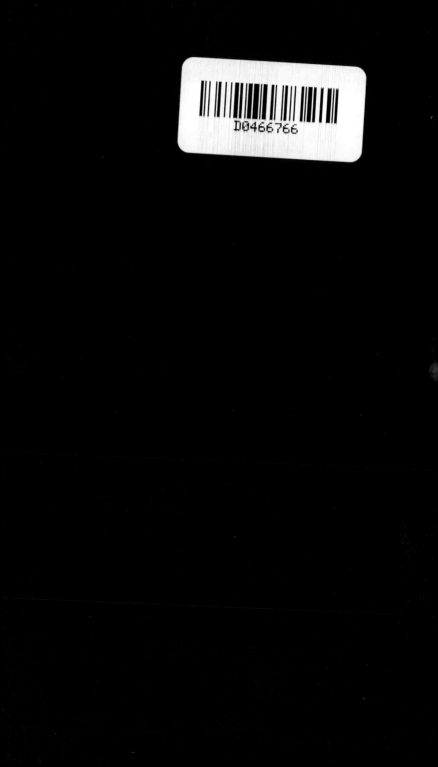

A CAGE IN SEARCH OF A BIRD

THE FRENCH LIST

FLORENCE NOIVILLE

A CAGE IN SEARCH OF A BIRD

TRANSLATED BY TERESA LAVENDER FAGAN

LONDON NEW YORK CALCUTTA

The work is published with the support of the
Publication Assistance Programmes of the Institut français /
French Ministry of foreign and European affairs

Seagull Books, 2016

© Éditions Stock, 2015

English translation © Teresa Lavender Fagan, 2016

ISBN   978 0 8574 2 375 7

British Library Cataloguing-in-Publication Data
A catalogue record for this book is available from the British Library.

Typeset by Seagull Books, Calcutta, India
Printed and bound by Maple Press, York, Pennsylvania, USA

'A cage went in search of a bird.'
Franz Kafka

'There is another world, but it is inside this one.'
Paul Eluard

Prologue

Are disorders of the soul in the order of things? Very ill people live among us, psychotics who pretend to be normal, because they don't want to be crazy. For the average person, if he or she isn't a victim, there are no visible symptoms. Our defences are down, we rub elbows with the unhinged. They might hold responsible jobs. It may even be the case that we like them. Until the day when the unhinged door falls off.

www.afp.comfr/societe/faitdivers—Friday, 23 June at 7.13 p.m., a woman fell from the roof terrace of the Hotel Molitor on rue Nungesser-et-Coli, near the Bois de Boulogne in Paris. The investigation will determine whether it was an accident, suicide or murder.

1

Something Is Wrong

That day I became convinced that something was wrong.

'Look! I'm dressed as you!'

C came into the room where I was working and made that statement, her voice filled with joy.

Even today I hear her throaty voice stressing the *you*. I should have looked up, but I let the words sink into my brain. There was something strange about them. Why 'as you', and not 'like you'? And the stress on *you*?

I finally looked away from my computer screen. And I saw her . . . 'as me'. The grey cashmere coat, the tight skirt, the silk blouse. Letting the effect of looking in a mirror sink in. A few days earlier she had complimented me on what I was wearing, asked me where I bought my clothes. So she must have bought the same ones. Exactly the same ones. Only her shoes were different. Extremely thin heels, slightly curved, much higher than I usually wear.

She walked back and forth in my office, slowly, without taking her eyes off me. Looking at me with an icy stare. I was incapable of uttering a word. I remember having the feeling that her statement sounded like a warning.

'I'm dressed as you.' See how easy it is for me to be you.

At that moment I felt a strange tingling in my fingers.

That day, I understood that something was wrong.

*

My name is Laura Wilmote. I'm a journalist. I work for a large television station whose very existence seems miraculous. At least to me. It's hard to express exactly how attached I feel to this profession. Not just because I find it useful, or because I am naturally a perfectionist and often stressed out—this is putting it mildly, as my fiancé, Eduardo, would say. It's just that my interview subjects rarely bore me. Artists, writers, thinkers, scientists . . . they follow one another in quick succession. Each time, my challenge is simple—to make them give a bit of themselves. Something emotional, something true. I don't like pomposity.

In the editing room, the technicians tell me that I do this very well. Sometimes the hair stylist or the make-up woman comes to watch the show—'It's a sign,' the director exclaims, delighted. 'For twenty-six minutes you really put the viewer into the skin of someone else. He enters an "experimental identity", a bit like one visits a model flat. What could be more exhilarating?'

Maybe what I experience is intense enough to be sufficient in itself. Off the set, I'm not very concerned with others. Not deliberately, though. Let's say that I'm on the sidelines, I slip by. I have friends, but they are very well selected. Sometimes I'm considered stuck up. Distant. Cold. That bothers me. I'm just solitary and discreet. At least I always had been until I encountered C.

I said I wasn't that concerned about others. That's not entirely true. In fact, nothing attracts me more than the 'Other'. To get in front of him. Not for a polite exchange but for a true encounter. 'Ready, Laura? Headphones, there, you hear me? 4-3-2-1. And go . . .' And we're off for 13 x 2 minutes during which I will attempt to plunge inside the guest, to swim with him in the deep end, to approach the shadowy depths of his anxieties, to travel along the weak lines, to explore his fears, elicit his memories, circumvent his secrets to better reveal them, find his wounds, inhibitions, disgusts, dreams, fantasies, pain, obsessions, destructions, frustrations, anger . . .

Very often—and this is true of all of us—only one of these emotions really count. The primal emotion. Everything turns around it and we return to it, as to a spring. It's up to me to detect it with my divining rod. If I don't sense anything, if nothing vibrates—emotion functions on the same basis as sound and light, vibrations—it's because I've understood nothing about the person who is sitting across from me. But if I'm allowed to get closer . . .

*

To understand, is that to 'stand with'? A bit like 'compassion'—or that funny word Balzac invented: *compatissance*—describes the ability to 'suffer with'? When the guest has the feeling he has been understood—I can see it in his eyes—he takes me with him. Includes me in a halo of gratitude and benevolence. I need that minute of grace. When, happy with his dive and return to the surface, the interviewee takes off his diving suit, breathes in a large gulp of oxygen and smiles at me. With an air of saying: 'If I had known . . . that all of that would take us so far . . . '

I smile, too. Not at him or at the camera. But at those moments when I am no longer alone. I have conquered the unhealthy timidity that enslaved me throughout my childhood. Constant apprehension. A lack of confidence. I have approached the Other. We have 'spoken together'. And our words had the exact weight of words. A miracle.

*

All of that really has very little to do with the media aspect of the thing. It is an intimate victory. People can't imagine just how vulnerable I was . . . before. When I was young, I never expressed myself, I never laughed. Seeking refuge in my books, dreams, nature, I liked to walk alone, barefoot, on the warm grass. Contemplative . . . between two shows, I go back to being like that. Perhaps because I have too much respect for language, I suffer during conversations when nothing is being said, when words turn on themselves, like in an empty tub of a washing machine. Washed out, deformed, with no more colour or shine. So I prefer to retreat. But no one seems to understand. Silence and solitude have become luxuries today. I am considered stuck up. 'Laura Wilmote, you know . . .'

*

My father was also a man of few words. Before he died, he quoted this marvellous saying to me: 'It is not proof of mental health to be perfectly at ease in a sick society.' He saw me, suffering from the same mis-understandings as he was, dragging my hyper-sensitivity around with me, paralysed by the gaze of others, lowering my eyes, hugging walls, fleeing contact and hating myself for it. It would have taken years of work on myself to overcome that. It's probably difficult to understand for anyone who hasn't gone through it. But to hold the gaze of someone without my heart beating out of my chest, to agree to be myself without pretending, just as I am, peaceful . . . yes, it would have taken me years to reach that balance.

Paradoxically, TV helped me. There's nothing like the conditions of live TV to confront 'danger'. I took the bull by the horns and I'm very proud of that. Today, I think I've won the match against myself. At least I thought so. Until I ran into C again.

*

When I think about the 'clothing scene', I say to myself that someone else might have smiled about it. Or even laughed. Why did I immediately sense something unsettling? Why was I ill at ease?

*

When I think about it, I also say to myself that there had been early warnings. Now I remember the time when I had thought I saw C at the Café des Arts, for example. At the TV station where C and I work, everyone goes to the Kobra. Not I. My usual neighbourhood is on the other side of the city. I'm sure I won't run into anyone there. I sit at my table. Always the same one. I immerse myself in the preparation of my show. I dive in. I'm somewhere else.

That week I was working on the theme of jealousy. A toxic passion. A poisoned elixir. Inadmissible, too. One can say: I am happy, sad, depressed, in love, furious, disappointed, nervous, preoccupied . . . no one will willingly tell you: I am jealous. It's an unspeakable feeling. Because, to the risk of being dropped or loved less is added that of being ridiculous; we don't speak of it. And it is exactly because we don't speak of it that I wanted to do a show on the subject.

*

So, on the first floor of the Café des Arts, I was drawing up a list of jealous people. Hera, Agrippina, Iago, Madame de Montespan . . . the great jealous people of history. I even thought of the French president's

9

former partner, Madame Trierweiler—her name had been in the papers that week—when the waitress came up to me . . . could I settle my tab? The room was emptying. I looked up and at that very moment I noticed a pump with very high heels quickly turning the corner in the room . . .

*

I was certain I had recognized that shoe. But why would C have gone to the trouble of coming all the way there? A work meeting? No one in our circle ever had meetings in this neighbourhood . . . Had she followed me? The next day, I had the impression I saw her again, not far from where I live near the Trocadéro. A hallucination? Foreboding? Something of C was prowling. As uncontrollable as a sail in the wind.

From that moment, a suspicion began to unfold inside me like a man-eating plant.

*

Also from that moment I began to understand what might have happened to me a few weeks earlier. I said I was a journalist, but I also write novels. These two activities satisfy my need for expression. The old media are enough for me. I don't use the so-called social networks. And yet, recently, people have been sending me bizarre emails. People I don't know thanking me for having 'friended' them—a term I've always found stupid. A certain Horacio Assuncao invited me to 'like Horacio Assuncao' and pointed out that four other friends 'liked' him. These people commented on photos of me that I was completely unaware of. Responded to something I had never said . . . At the beginning it made me smile. Then it became disturbing. I went to the station's IT department where I explained my problem. 'You see,' I said to the technician, 'I'm not on Facebook, I haven't asked anyone to do anything . . .'

'Yes you are,' he interrupted me, 'you have an account you don't know about. Someone created it for you. And this someone who isn't you is speaking through you. Do you have any idea who that could be?'

*

At the time I had no idea. But later, C's statement came back to me. You see how easy it is for me to be you. The heady and horrifying idea of the interchangeability of people started to churn in my head. C had created this fake account to be 'even more me'? A space to which, ironically, I didn't have access and where surely she was having me say . . . what could she be having me say?

*

Absurd. What if I was just making all this up? Too much work, too much stress. Imagination running wild. 'You're working too hard . . . ' I heard Eduardo say, 'Slow down, Bebita . . . why don't you and I go on a holiday? You could come with me to Mexico.' Eduardo's great fantasy—that we leave together and settle down in his native land.

*

Had I dreamt it all? Independently of C, I have always had a tendency to think that facts are never 'true' in themselves. They simply punctuate our fantasies. Films that we create for ourselves. Stories that we tell ourselves . . .

And yet, shortly after the clothing scene, my phone rang in the middle of the night.

'My cell phone vibrated . . . ' C said in a voice that was cooler than usual. 'I knew right away it was you . . . '

Knew it was I? I made an enormous effort to pull myself out of sleep and stupor. But even though I tried to tell her it was impossible, that I was asleep, that I hadn't called anyone, C persisted. She said it was me. She knew.

What the hell did she know?

I listened to her breathing into the phone. Not broken, but full and determined. After a silence she said she knew how much I needed her. She understood.

She repeated that, several times. Clearly detaching her words. She knew, she understood. She seemed completely awake. She added that she was there. That she would always be there for me. That I didn't need to be afraid.

*

I wasn't afraid. Not yet. My only fear was that this nonsense would end up waking Eduardo. I saw him rolled up in the sheet. Next to me. His back turned to me. His wide, brown shoulders rising and falling in rhythm. His lips parted, softly whistling. Luckily, he seemed to be asleep.

'We have to talk,' said C.

To talk? But about what? What?

I suddenly realized that the tingling—that bizarre tingling—had started again with a vengeance. As if hundreds of thousands of ants had made nests in my fingers.

I wanted to yell. I yelled in a whisper that I had not called her. That she was out of her mind. That it was crazy to call people like that for nothing in the middle of the night. If there were a problem she had only to say so. To stop acting like this. Stop following me. Stop opening false accounts on Facebook for me.

There was silence. At that moment Eduardo turned over, probably in search of a cooler spot for his cheek on the pillow. I hung up, then turned off my phone.

*

That night I had to take a pill to go back to sleep. But C returned in my dreams. She was standing very straight on the tips of her heels and brandishing a butcher's knife. She laughed her forced laugh and repeated that I shouldn't be afraid. Because she was there. And she wasn't going to leave me. Never leave me again.

*

It was early the next day when Eduardo left the house. As usual, he was in a hurry. He was flying off to Mexico. I couldn't talk to him about anything. He is always a bit distracted when he travels on business. When he kissed me goodbye I was still in bed, cloudy with the effects of the sleeping pill. Little by little, pieces of the dream floated to the surface. Black and putrid pieces of old, floating wood.

*

That day I couldn't stop going over the sequence of events. 'I'm dressed as you.' Facebook. The call in the middle of the night. The absurd, incoherent speech. And that striking and persistent impression of being followed, spied on, watched. I wrote all that down in a black notebook. I like making notes of what I can't explain. That's how my novels are born. To explain to myself things that I don't understand.

*

And I really don't understand what is happening to C. We were both eighteen when we met for the first time. It was in a class we were taking at a high school in the Latin Quarter. She had gone to that school in the city for many years; I had just arrived from the provinces, and was a boarder. The first day, in the second row, we were sitting side by side. I, a newbie, introverted. She, with a colourful vocabulary and loose tongue. I can still see her—a tall brunette with slightly-wide-set black eyes. Lots of energy. And full of attention for me, which surprised me right away.

*

Sometimes, on the weekend, she insisted on inviting me to her parents' shop—it would be good to get out. They had a butcher shop on place de la Contrescarpe. She explained the knives to me: the slicing knives, the boning knives, the cleavers. Made me admire the carcasses in the cold room. 'Hard as marble . . . and the colours . . . look . . . like Soutine's slab of raw beef . . .'

*

She introduced me to that painter and to many others. Above the butcher shop, in her room, we would talk late into the night. Thanks to her, I belatedly discovered New Wave cinema, and Antonioni, and Satyajit Ray . . . C had read a lot, she was informed, lively and intelligent. But what surprised me the most was that she had become my friend. I, the timid one, the girl who felt completely at ease only in her own company. I, who up to then loved to be alone, to meditate, daydream . . . and now, without realizing it . . . how can I put it? She hadn't 'asked' me but, rather, 'kidnapped me as a friend'. I had been ravished in both senses of the term.

*

I discovered connection, the complicity of friends. Happiness in the company of another. I was attracted to her. Her eyes, her spirit. For the first time, I wasn't alone, and it felt good. What others had taken as aloofness she had understood as something else. She had been able to uncover my secret weakness, and I was grateful to her. I felt changed, at peace.

*

C stimulated me. 'What, you've never read Pindar? Sappho? . . . Come on, take that . . .' She threw two books at me, laughing. 'And then, first of all, take . . . *La Couronne et la Lyre* . . .' Books were flying around her room. That evening, in my little boarding student cell, I drank them in eagerly. I was doing better in class.

*

One day, one of us had fallen upon a scene in a novel in which two characters were playing a game of truth. Each person took a sheet of paper that was torn in two. 'What I like about you.' 'What I don't like about you.' We wanted to play it, too. To tell each other everything. At the time, I was incapable of filling out the second sheet. She, too . . . That day we had put on some music—Nina Simone. We laughed. And even danced. I was sitting next to her on the bed. 'My baby don't care . . . ' We were eighteen.

*

(Years later, in the television station office, C reminded me of that scene. I admit that, until she brought it up, I had completely forgotten about it.)

*

At the end of the year, our paths diverged. I passed our exams, she failed. It was unfair—she should have passed.

*

More than me, perhaps ... ?

*

I went to live on the school campus. She registered at the public university. We lost touch.

*

An injustice. When I think back on it, that's putting it mildly ... On the ancient literature exam, there was a question on Pindar's *Dithyramb for Athens*. I owed her a huge debt, and she knew it. I can still see her look when the results were announced. Disappointment, bitterness. As if she, the daughter of butchers, was silently thinking: 'Always the same ones ...'

*

I saw her years later in a bookstore in Paris. I was signing books. She had seen the poster and she had come. Did I have time for a coffee?

In the cafe I noticed that she hadn't changed much. Still extroverted, voluble, warm. But much better dressed than in our high-school days. She was wearing brown crocodile pumps with pointed toes and very high heels. It was the first time I saw her like that, refined, feminine. And life? She frowned. No boyfriend . . . Well—brief hesitation—an unhappy experience, very unhappy, which had hurt her . . . She would tell me about it . . . And as far as work was concerned, she was vegetating as a freelancer at a woman's magazine. She envied my job. If I ever heard of an opening at the station . . .

*

Looking back, I tell myself everything is my fault. I threw open the gates of the sheep pen to the wolf. That is, if you can compare the sharks at the TV station to sheep . . . but many are both at the same time, sharks up to their jaws, and sheep in their heads . . . Also, I didn't really deserve to be there. When I heard of a job opening, a job as a journalist in the news department, I called her right away.

*

Looking back, I think I can also say that I felt guilty. I had a diffuse sense of guilt, buried for years, but which our recent meeting brought back to the surface.

Everything she had given me during exam preparations—everything, without intending to, I had taken from her—Pindar, the Greeks, the test, the school, the diploma—I wanted to repair the injustice. Wasn't this the perfect opportunity?

*

C was hired. And the graft took. She was immediately a hit at the station, very charming. Liked and appreciated by everyone. As for us, at least I believed this, we had become friends again.

*

But in retrospect, two things now occur to me. C was charming, but I remember she called me at home when I had something, nothing serious, a simple cold . . . I remember thinking several times: 'She's doing too much.' It was a fleeting thought. I had probably pushed it away then, mad at myself for being myself. Too harsh.

*

I also remember, but again, after the fact, the strange relationships she maintained with my family. She had run into my mother in the past. Now, she wanted to see her again and get to know everyone, my brothers, my sisters, my friends. She flattered them. She made them laugh. She had a knack for getting herself invited everywhere. She was pleasant, amusing. She was invited back . . . Gradually, my world became hers. I didn't notice a thing.

*

One day my mother said something about her: 'Your friend C is sweet . . . it's amazing how much she admires you. I tried to brush off a compliment and go on to another subject, but she kept heaping praise on you. She kept repeating that you were successful in anything you undertook—school, the TV station, Eduardo, your books . . . She even said, "You know, Laura is not just a good journalist, she's a novelist, that is . . . the books she's written, I'm maybe a bit jealous. I would have liked to have written them . . . "'

*

'I would have liked to have written them . . . ' I was just thinking about that when I realized it was incredibly late. Two in the morning. I had let my thoughts wander off. I was about to go to bed when the phone rang.

C. She said the same incomprehensible things she had said when she called before: 'Don't be afraid. I'll be there for you. I'll never let you go again . . . ' I didn't have the strength to listen to that babbling any more. I hung up and silenced my phone. From now on, I said to myself, I'll turn my phone off before I go to bed. I'll let Eduardo know so he won't be worried. I'll unplug. I'll have peace. Except that . . . a journalist that can't be reached? What would happen if something urgent came up at the station? I'm not taking things seriously? I'm not a professional?

*

At the station, my office opens onto a hallway. Or, rather, one of the walls is along the hallway. It's a cloudy glass wall, except for the lower fifty centimetres off the ground where the glass is transparent. Ever since the scene with the outfit, C has been deliberately passing along the wall of my office. Several times a day she walks by, in one direction or the other, slowly. Abnormally slowly. I don't see her exactly, but

I recognize her legs. Cut-off legs that seem to want to touch me from behind the glass. Sections of legs that come and go with calm determination. Seeming to say: 'Follow me, come on, follow me . . . ' Or something even stranger. I follow a ballet of calves with troubling fascination. The tips of her heels plunge like a knife into the soft carpet.

*

My show is to air in less than a week. I'm late. I must work. Not think of her any more. Concentrate. Concentrate. Maybe I should reread *Phaedra*? When she is rejected by Hippolytus, Theseus' wife accuses him of all sorts of betrayal and has him executed. Will that work with my subject? I have to be careful not to be too literary. Not to neglect the scientific, more modern dimension . . . My colleague in the documentation department has prepared a large, red file on jealousy. Very serious articles in which the same words constantly appear: rivalry, persecution, harassment, power, narcissism, brother complex . . . There is also that article in a woman's magazine on 'toxic friends'. This involves true friendships, but which are ruined because of resentment or things left unsaid then transformed into destructive duos. A woman called Eva says, 'Because of her, I lost my confidence. By stealing my life, my friends, controlling my relationship, she ended up making me feel worthless.'

*

Toxic friends. Seeing that word, I'm suddenly eight or nine years old again. In her pharmacy which smells like eau de cologne, I hear my mother shout, 'The toxics . . . has anyone seen the key to the toxics?' At the time, I only knew that they were rare and venomous substances that were lined up in a row on the shelves of a small cabinet also called 'Table B'. That they were handled with extreme caution. Then they were replaced as quickly as possible into the cabinet which was immediately locked up. I couldn't imagine that that label could be applied to anything other than chemical products. Beings who were sufficiently harmful that one would want to lock them up in a cabinet and throw away the key.

*

In that magazine article, another woman said, 'Gabrielle was my best friend for ten years. We worked together, we were neighbours, talked all the time. When I tried to break away from her influence, I hurt her feelings. The result was she did the most horrible thing she could—she slept with my husband.'

*

C came to dinner once or twice at my place. Then she invited us back. She was charming and seductive with Eduardo, as she can be with everyone. But from that to wanting to sleep with him . . . Anyway, I'm the one she calls during the night. I who mustn't be afraid. I whom she follows everywhere. I whom she wants to 'protect'.

*

Let's go back to the beginning. How to explain C's abrupt metamorphosis? What led her to want to 'be me' to the point of stealing my appearance, my outfits, my friends, to act like me, to be me on Facebook? Jealousy? I naturally think that's it because of my TV show. Does C want to be me because she covets the things I have? What can she be envious of ? I keep thinking of that phrase of the Tao: 'I compete with no one, so no one can compete with me.'

*

There is something else. Something that right now I can't explain.

2

De Clérambault's Syndrome

I can't remember how the idea came to me—probably from my show. I call Pierre-Henri from my office. PH agrees to see me in-between two patients. I go to his office, on rue Soufflot. A luxurious room, plush sofa, kilims, lamps emitting soft light. That's where I learn about de Clérambault for the first time.

*

Gaëtan Gatian de Clérmbault was a French psychiatrist born in 1872 in Bourges and who died in Malakoff in 1934. In 1902, de Clérambault was an intern at the special infirmary of the Paris police headquarters. He became the head physician there around twenty years later. Each year, in the department of emergency admissions of the mentally ill, he saw thousands of people whose mental illness 'disturbed the public order'. He was particularly interested in cases of romantic delusions, a pathology that he described in detail, and which henceforth bore his name: de Clérambault's Syndrome.

*

I ask PH how he would describe the syndrome, exactly. 'What? The syndrome?'

He rubs his thick moustache. Did he have it at the time we used to meet? I want to take some scissors and clean it up a bit.

'De Clérambault called it "the delusional illusion of being loved".'

'Tell me more, PH . . . I could use a good lecture on de Clérambault . . . '

He smiles. It's getting dark outside. 'How to begin? OK, here I go . . . ' And he points at a street lamp that has just turned on across the street. 'One day,' he says, 'the patient has a revelation. He goes from darkness to light. He suddenly becomes convinced that he is loved. Loved by . . . "the Object".'

'But what makes him suddenly convinced of that?'

'Nothing—that's the point. It takes nothing . . . Someone you see at the bus stop can trigger de Clérambault Syndrome . . . that's why there's no way to anticipate it. Nor to prevent it.'

'Can you give me an example?'

'What can I tell you . . . The typical case is that of X who one day goes to a Johnny Hallyday, or some other concert by a popular singer. And there—surprise!—while Johnny is moving around on the stage, his eyes meet those of X. Yes, he, Johnny, the singer. His gaze lingers on X and he winks at him. X experiences that as something incredible, you can imagine . . . "I would never have thought that Johnny would give me a sign! It's crazy . . . And yet, I'm not mistaken, doctor, he really looked at me and winked his right eye . . . "'

'Then what?'

'Then that's when the problems start. X tells you, "I know you won't believe me, doctor. But I swear, Johnny winked at me. At me. There's no doubt . . . He was on stage . . . "'

*

Is it possible that C thinks that I love her? For PH it's perfectly possible. I'm in shock.

*

De Clérambault. What was he like, the man of the syndrome? On the Internet he has a round, bald head. A well-trimmed moustache above thin lips and then, beneath his spectacles, heavy eyelids that fall over his eyes. They give him a strange look. A mix of distance and authority.

*

Will he be able to provide me with the key? Since I began taking notes in my little Moleskine notebook, the idea of a novel emerged. It's taking root in my head. Every evening I look deeper into the subject with, I must admit, a certain amount of exaltation. This pathology is fascinating. The fact that Eduardo is in Mexico actually turns out to be a good thing.

*

Like Freud with Anna, de Clérambault has 'his' case. The case of Léa. Financially comfortable, well-spoken Léa, fifty-three years old, arrived at the special infirmary one grey December day in 1920. De Clérambault was immediately interested in her because of what he called 'the prideful constructions of her imagination'.

What did she say? That the king of England, George V, was madly in love with her. That, for two years, he has continued to make advances towards her. That he has sent countless emissaries to her, English

or American officers for the most part. Or even someone close to General Lyautey. A man who, one day, in a
train, told her 'a thousand things in code'. Alas, she
only understood too late the secret meaning of his
words.

For some time, Georges V himself has crossed her
path. A bit like Zeus with his future conquests, he
appears to her in unexpected disguises. One day as a
tourist, the next day as a sailor. It also happens that he
appears as himself, but only furtively. Like that night
when Léa was sleeping in an expensive hotel in
London and she heard someone knocking at her door.
It must have been 11 p.m. The time it took her to put
on a robe . . . the visitor was gone. Who else could it
have been? It had to have been George. It had to have
been HIM.

*

What's striking about this psychosis is the power
of the hallucination. The suddenness of its onset.
OFF/ON. Like a switch you turn on or off. An emotional switch.

*

'Another question,' I say to PH. 'Johnny has just winked at X . . . What happens next?'

'Next, it's very simple. Even very logical. X will try to contact Johnny, because Johnny is calling to him. He will go to another concert . . . "Because you can't take me for a fool, doctor. I saw what I saw . . . " X wants to make sure. He returns to the concert to see if the same thing will happen. And unfortunately it does happen again—at least in general. Or if it doesn't happen again, X is in any case changed for ever. Incapable of thinking of anything else. Incapable of thinking in any other way. "It happened so clearly . . . you understand, doctor?" '

'You mean that in X's mind there is truly no possible ambiguity?'

'None at all. For the patient, what happened is there. Real. Huge. As unequivocal as a large boulder in the middle of his backyard. How can I explain it . . . it's as if X were suddenly flooded with certainty. Johnny winked at me, Johnny loves me, Johnny wants me. It is a non-dialectic love. An emotion of incredible violence.'

*

I'm listening to PH and thinking of C. I ask him how he deals with his 'de Clérambault patients'. He says that the main challenge is not to enter into their delusion while being perfectly aware that what they are experiencing is 'real'.

*

Back home, I'm exhausted, I have doubts. 'Stop jumping to conclusions,' an English friend is always telling me. Can it be that all of this is simply—as de Clérambault would put it—a 'prideful construction of my imagination'?

*

Wouldn't it be best simply to talk directly with C? I screw up my courage and leave her a message. Why don't we talk things over seriously? In the day rather than at night? Ten minutes later C calls back. She says she agrees, 'of course she agrees'. We set a meeting for the next day, at a cafe near the Trocadéro. That evening I dive back into de Clérambault.

*

Léa explained to de Clérambault how angry she was at herself for having recognized her beloved king only after the fact. Obviously, that was why she didn't immediately respond to his advances. It was also why, in her opinion, he was angry at her.

To make amends, she increased her trips to London. She spent a lot of money to be in the train stations where the king 'planned to meet her'. She spent hours in front of the gates of Buckingham Palace. One day when she was looking at the windows of the palace, she saw a curtain move. No mistake, her beloved was indeed watching her. Once again, he was trying to get in touch with her. He had signalled her. In the face of so many advances, Léa was in seventh heaven. She felt happiness wash over her. Later, de Clérambault would have a name for that phase of the illness. He called it the 'state of ardent expectation'.

*

At the Trocadéro cafe, that's exactly what C explains to me. That she senses happiness getting closer. That it is there, within reach. Why would I refuse it? Then she repeats what she said on the phone—that I don't need to be afraid. That she understood. I had so clearly signalled to her that night. I was so moving and beautiful, the day of that signing . . .

The day of the signing? I understand that she's talking about the encounter around my last novel that took place a few days earlier in a bookstore. She says, 'Remember, you talked about the weight of conventions, the weight of forbidden love. Of what happens in us when we fall in love with someone we should never have approached.' She explains that she came to see me at the end of the presentation, to have me sign the book. And that it was there, when I handed it to her, that I looked at her in a certain way . . .

'A long look,' she says, 'like a beckoning . . .'

She repeats that I mustn't be afraid. That it's all very natural.

*

On rue Soufflot, PH advises me to flee. With de Clérambaults, he says, there's nothing to be done. Except to immediately break all ties. I show him my little notebook and explain that it's impossible. I want to approach that parallel world where C has perhaps gone, and into which she is trying to draw me. Can he help me?

*

An email from C:

'I know what you're feeling, Laura. Love between women is still unsettling, even more than that between men. The truth is that boys and girls love the same. We're no longer in the time of Lucie Delarue-Mardrus. Or of the Duchess of Polignac. When women who loved women had to marry men to have social status. Open your eyes, Laura. The path is no longer forbidden. I'll help you . . . Help you to be you.'

*

I am me. She's the one who is no longer the same. And it is precisely that which frightens me and intrigues me at the same time. I tell PH again what I hope to do with my novel—enter C's delusion. Visit her psychosis. Since C claims to know better than I that I love her, to have direct access to my emotions, I will do the same. Journey into her brain like a writer travelling on a research trip. Then I ask him again: Can he help me?

*

Psychiatrists are always crazier than you think. PH wants to help. He can put me in touch with the parents of one of his young patients, Alexia. 'A pure de

Clérambault . . . but only for the needs of the novel . . . you'll change the names, I'm sure.' He shrugs his shoulders and raises his eyes to the heavens. He adds that even when I was a student, I was stubborn. Then he tells me that de Clérambault was a great psychiatrist, but a very short man. Behind his desk at the special infirmary he had had his chair discreetly raised to be at the same level as those he was speaking to. He wore high-heeled boots and, when he was standing, his white coat reached his knees. And so? So nothing.

*

C's emails are getting stranger and stranger:

'Laura, in your new existence there will no longer be room for any doubt. I will be there and will protect you. I will enfold you or, rather, you will enfold yourself with me. Another woman will meet you, Laura. Tomorrow you will be Another. Hold out your hand to that Other.'

*

De Clérambault speaking of Léa: 'The only motive for her certainty was her emotion.' Just as we speak of anxiety attacks, the psychiatrist has a nice expression for crises such as Léa's: 'Hope Attacks.'

*

Alexia's parents. I speak to them on the phone. I tell them the truth. I say I'm planning to write a novel involving de Clérambault's Syndrome. I say I'm hoping to meet their daughter. Why not, they answer. They will ask her if she would be willing. Adding that with Alexia, you never knew . . .

*

In the end, Alexia agrees to see me.

When I am sitting across from her I feel completely at a loss. As if I hadn't done hundreds of interviews for television. I start in the simplest of ways:

'How are you?'

'I have anxiety attacks. In the morning, when I wake up, I don't know where I am. I feel like someone is watching me. I'm really afraid.'

Alexia has round, smooth cheeks. How old could she be? Thirty? Thirty-five? Her parents warned me.

She had been pretty before she started taking medication. Her voice has still retained a childlike tone. Especially when she said, so quietly, 'I'm really afraid.'

'Afraid?'

'Patrick Bruel has been watching me for twenty years. We met . . . and even though I didn't want to go out with him, he still wants to know everything about me, without telling me . . . '

She's looking at me and I can't believe it. The case PH described is taking sharp shape right in front of me.

'No, I didn't want to go out with him . . . The age difference was too big. We didn't have the same religion. Plus, he's famous, and that scared me.'

'He's the one who wanted to go out with you?'

'It wasn't clear. We met through a common friend. We spoke on the phone, he was working on an album . . . Everything began very simply, you know. My sister gave me a ticket to one of his concerts, and I remember telling myself, "He's a good singer, very down-to-earth, why not . . . " After the concert, thanks to our common friend, we spoke a bit. Then I called him back. I suggested we go to an exhibition, but he said he was working on an album.'

'Was he avoiding you?'

'He was ambivalent, he wanted . . . even now he's ambivalent. He doesn't know what he wants. For example . . . he doesn't want me to meet his sons. He's very protective. Even so . . . I'd really like to get to know them. Even if being in a relationship with someone who has kids is frightening.'

'Do you think about him a lot?'

'All the time, since I know he's watching me.'

There's a pause, then a change of tone.

'My life has changed, I no longer have a social life,' Alexia continues, angry now. 'You can't just film people like that. It's an invasion of privacy. I've contacted his lawyer. I've even gone to see a *procureur*. I've had to put up curtains everywhere in my house. I can only live behind closed curtains. It's really awful.'

'Are you angry at him?'

'Of course I am!' she says, raising her voice, 'He's ruining my life, that's what he's doing.'

When I ask her whether she's still in love with him, Alexia bursts into tears.

'It's like a break-up that won't end. The separations are always painful. This has been going on for twenty years . . . '

One day Alexia had tried to confide in her best friend. But, she says, even friends can't understand. They are powerless. She repeats that word: powerless.

She tells me how alone she feels: 'Du côté noir, du côté froid.' She listens to that every day on YouTube. She watches clips of concerts taken by fans. She's signed up on his website. She recalls every one of his photos, doesn't miss any opportunity to see him on television, knows his concert dates by heart.

She talks to him and answers him in a song:

'Which one of you, which one of me will have been wrong? Which one of us will say, I still believe?'

'See, he's sending me messages. He's proving he still loves me.'

'But . . . these are questions . . . do you think he's asking himself the same thing?'

Alexia looks at me for a long moment. Her eyes are saying, 'Why are you asking me that when you *know* that I'm right?'

'That's right,' she concludes, 'You've understood everything.'

*

That night, at home, I'm sitting immobile on a kitchen stool. Astounded by the power of the illusion. The delusional illusion of being loved. I have a thought that goes round and round in my head. Like on a Formula One racetrack. For more than twenty years.

An out-of-control racecar. And Alexia no longer has the key to turn off the engine.

*

I write that thought down in my little black notebook: Delusional Illusion of Being Loved. An *idée fixe*. Intractable. I play with this notion like a word game.

An IDEA. Incomprehensible. Destruction. Exasperation. Anguish . . . Impotence. Dispossession. Enfold. Alienation . . . And at the same time in me: Interest (Intellectual). Desire (to know more). Enthusiasm (to have a good subject). Ambiguity (will I be taking a risk here?). In sum, the Unreasonable Impression of Being Elsewhere (above any danger).

*

The phone rings.

C again?

I jump back a foot or so, as if a snake were sitting there, coiled, on the kitchen table. I approach the phone with caution. It's Eduardo. Yes, he arrived safely. 'Of course, Bebita . . . Stop worrying about everything . . . ¿Y tu, mi amor . . . cómo estás?'

When Eduardo starts speaking Spanish, it means he's tired. Jetlagged. I have a burning desire to tell him everything. My discovery of de Clérambault. That mix of fear and excitement I feel. That I think I have the subject of my next book . . .

But now is not the time. Not on the phone. Not at a distance of over five thousand miles. So I say as calmly as I can that all is well. All is very well . . . 'Eduardo . . . ?' 'Yes?' 'When will you be home?'

*

Before turning off the light I look at my email one more time. C has written:

'It is while we fight, Laura, while dreaming of the Utopia that you and I will build our life together. There was a fire in your eyes at the Trocadéro cafe. Come to me, Laura. Free yourself into my confidence.'

*

Irritating. Demented. Exasperating. Acidic.

3

Voyage to the Centre of the Delusion

A few days later, I show PH my notes on Alexia. 'What strikes me,' he says, 'is that one might say she is a psychotic who is trying not to seem crazy.' I ask him what he means by that. 'Who knows what she was doing just an hour before talking to you,' he says. 'Maybe she was lying in front of Bruel's door? Maybe she was sending him erotic or pornographic messages? When you go to an erotomaniac's—or a "de Clérambault", as you call them—you might find wastebaskets filled with letters. One day I found seven thousand . . . '

'So?'

'Alexia didn't know you. She spoke to you in a controlled way. That means one thing: erotomaniacs aren't crazy. You see what I mean? They know very well they are taking a huge risk. They have absolutely no intention of ending up in jail. You're a professional interviewer, you got her to confide in you. She told you that Bruel was talking in her head, calling to her. But she didn't want to go too far. With someone else she might not have shown anything at all. Appear perfectly normal.'

He rubs his moustache.

'Many de Clérambault patients try to avoid being found out,' he says. 'They exhibit a great deal of caution. At the TV station, doesn't your C appear completely normal?'

*

Our patient, Léa, was brought to us for a rather ordinary reason. Having returned from London the day before, and unhappy with the apparent indifference of His Majesty, she was in an Underground train when she saw herself surrounded and mocked. She got out of the car very irritated. In the street she went up to two plainclothes policemen, scolded them for looking at her, for being good-for-nothings, and slapped them . . . Her family came to get her (brother-in-law and niece), Léa showed an extraordinary talent for lying. No sooner was she in front of them, smiling broadly, and with the most normal shows of affection, she started improvising, quickly and abundantly, a story explaining what she was doing in the special infirmary. She had fallen ill and had to be taken to the station, and she was sent here to be cured, which indeed happened. Etc. We would have been duped by her apparent candour, as well, if we didn't know about her.

(G. de Clérambault and Brousseau. *Bul. Soc.*
Clin. Ment., Dec. 1920, p. 238.)

*

Alexia, Léa and probably C. To see from the inside
what is going on in their sick minds. I think again of
Eduardo, who is not a scientist, but who has always
dreamt that someone, one day, would connect psychoanalysis and neurobiology. He told me so shortly after
we met for the first time. He was persuaded—and still
is—that one of the great challenges of the future will
be the interaction of those two disciplines. I talked
about this to the novelist Ian McEwan, who wrote on
de Clérambault Syndrome, and whom I interviewed
one day for the station. He thinks that's right. PH
shrugs his shoulders. 'The neurosciences have nothing
to say on your subject.'

*

Is that really true? I still want to test this theory. I
explain that I'm writing a book on de Clérambault
Syndrome and I set up a meeting in a large hospital in
Paris, at the Brain and Bone Marrow Institute. In the
waiting room, I study a cross-section of the nervous

system. I travel along the longitudinal fissure, the cortex, swim in white matter. I'm about to reach the central grey matter when the door opens. A man in jeans, with a relaxed manner, walks towards me, smiling. 'Hello,' says Dr M, holding out his hand.

*

Dr M is a specialist in obsessive-compulsive disorders. Why OCDs? 'Quite simply because for neurobiologists romantic obsessions are very close to obsessive-compulsive disorders,' he explains. 'You've come to the right person for your novel . . . ' He tells me that biologists have measured the concentration of a protein in the blood called serotonin transporter. 'This protein is present in the blood, but also in the brain where it regulates the concentration of serotonin, that messenger that influences mood and behaviour. Scientists have carried out studies over three groups— "normal" people, subjects that are "madly in love for a short amount of time" and patients who are victims of compulsive disorders. The results? They observed an analogous variation of the serotonin transporter in those recently in love and in patients with OCD.' I ask him what he concludes from this. 'Oh, quite simply that, for the neurosciences, to be madly in love is anything but a figure of speech.'

*

I don't tell him about C, but I ask him about the 'delusional illusion of being loved'. 'Ah,' he says, still smiling, 'good old de Clérambault . . . Well, it's pretty much the same thing, you see. The constant return of an obsessive image . . . to be haunted by the thought of not having locked the door, by the constant need to wash your hands, or by the certainty that someone loves you—in each case the subject is bombarded by intrusive and recurrent images. In every case the same phenomenon is produced in his brain. Which phenomenon? It's hard to say, exactly. But we can assume that certain groups of neurons are activated in a repeated and uncontrollable way.' Dr M talks about a feedback loop passing through the central grey matter, the cortex and the thalamus. A loop that continuously reactivates the activity of one of those groups of neurons. I mention my Formula One track. 'That's not such a bad image,' he says, obviously to humour me.

*

A new email from C:

'I've thought so much about you the past few days, my dear Laura. I should say the past few nights, too.

Guess what I've done! I asked the documentation department for recordings of all your shows. I watched them one after the other. Your presence surrounded me. You were there, Laura, it was lovely, it was warm. Mainly, I listened to the past . . . Heard the messages you sent me between the lines. How lucky I was to come listen to you at the bookstore the other evening! Everything suddenly became clear. Everything was obvious . . . I know you're going through some difficult times, Laura. We are all pulled apart from the inside. But I told you. I won't let you fall. For your show, too. I'm going to help you. I'm here, Laura. You'll see. You can count on me. C.

P.S. We have so much to talk about. Let's get together again. At the Trocadéro cafe?'

*

There aren't that many victims of de Clérambault Syndrome, at least not enough to merit an in-depth study, Dr M explained to me. Yet I'm shocked by the number of people around me who, either close or at a distance, have had experiences like mine.

*

'Do you remember my first wife, Ulrica?' my friend Vincent asks me. 'It was right after she was hired as a professor at the Sorbonne. Every day a guy came to talk to her after her classes, then followed her in the street. She found notes rolled up and stuffed in the keyhole at home. One day she read an anti-Semitic allusion on one of them. She finally spoke to me about it, and I picked up my phone and called the guy. I told him that if he continued I would call the police. Two days later I saw an announcement of his death in *Le Monde*—suicide.'

*

Why does C want to help me with my show? I've been doing this show for years and don't need any help. Then why? My perception of things is becoming unclear. Everything is jumbled up, cloudy like a blurry photo.

*

I agree to meet her at the cafe. Is it for the novel? I barely sit down, take off my raincoat—'A double espresso, please'—when she says, staring at me, 'Do you remember Sappho?'

Silence. I must look surprised. That was so long ago . . .

I understand that she's talking about that youthful attraction—fleeting and now very distant—that we experienced in high school. I admit that I had completely forgotten about it. I went on to other things. I even find the memory slightly funny . . .

*

Not her.

She repeats the question, and I burst out laughing.

*

At that moment, I can see in her eyes that that wasn't the right response at all. That she was expecting something else. Later, I would come to realize that something had been 'settled' then, in the past. At the time of Nina Simone. In high school. It had been dormant and then reawakened the evening of the bookstore. What did PH say? A fact. A fact as tangible as a stone in the middle of a garden: C is persuaded that I love her. That I have always loved her. How could I pretend to have forgotten?

*

I dive back into my research. I'm no longer interested in anything but de Clérambault Syndrome. I can feel the novel taking shape. I need material. In Eduardo's absence I see only people who have 'gone through it'.

*

When we meet at the restaurant, Riccardo, who is a surgeon, tells me that for a year he's been going through a terrible time. Persecuted by one of his former patients. It's somewhat his fault. Riccardo is a womanizer, he knows that. So? So, he operated on her. Saved her. But he clearly didn't cut things off soon enough afterwards. She started to come see him at the hospital, to bring him 'gifts', to follow his children on the way to school, to call him constantly. Why didn't he change his number? Riccardo tells me that in stalking cases, you have to be firm, not to enter into the stalker's game. I ask him if he is ever afraid. 'It's not really fear,' he says. 'Rather a sense of disorientation. You know me, I'm super-rational. In every situation I plan a strategy.' Riccardo draws arrows on the paper tablecloth. 'ABCD . . . I go from one point to another knowing very well where I want to end up. But here, nothing. I can't come up with any response.' He's silent for some time, then adds, 'I'm guessing you experience that, too. That strange feeling of weakness. Not physical weakness, but an undefined malaise. A slight panic. The disturbing surprise of finding yourself in *flagrante delicto* of a non-response . . . Never would I have thought that I would find myself like this, without a reaction, on the brink of the void.'

*

So something must have been fixed in C that was reawakened the night of the book signing. Something subconscious, perhaps, but in any case, unalterable.

'I hurt her,' I tell myself as I'm leaving the cafe.

I think about what she had told me the night at the bookstore. Her life at the university. A great heartbreak. Although C isn't unattractive, far from it. Brilliant, seductive, feminine. Charming, even magnetic. But she piles up failures. And here, without wanting to, I have just inflicted another wound, a wound to her self-esteem.

*

I had wanted to help her by getting her a job at the station. Erase my debt. Be even. But in that gesture, she must have seen an additional sign of my love for her. A love that I've turned into a joke. That I've reduced to nothing . . . Why are my actions and my words so contradictory? Am I toying with her?

*

'She had found my home address,' Riccardo tells me. 'She rang the bell and said to my wife through the intercom, "I have an appointment with Dr D . . . " One day she showed up at my office. I don't know how she was able to get past the reception desk. When I opened the door, she was there with a huge dog on a leash. I really thought I was a goner. That my final hour had come. That the monster was going to go for my throat . . . But . . . she just looked at me for a long time. Then she said, "I wanted my dog to get to know you."'

*

An email from C:

'It's always the same, Laura. You approach me, then you reject me. Do you think I've forgotten? How I helped you get into your school? And how, already, you made me understand you were interested in me . . . Interested, that's the right word. Interest, calculation is never absent in you, Laura. I understand that now. You used me. To get into that fucking school.

What about me? Pressured, then kicked to the kerb. Garbage. A butcher's daughter, basically . . . is that what you thought?

'Because you got me into the TV station, you think you don't owe me anything any more? Is that what you want me to believe?'

*

Two minutes later, another email from C:

'I'm not dreaming, Laura. That disturbing love, so pure, so deep, is still there. Intact. I can see it in your eyes, I recognize it, even hidden, in all the signs you send me.

'You hurt me at the cafe, but I thought about it. I forgive you. In the name of our relationship. In the name of Sappho. Deep down I know that you're pretending to have forgotten. You don't forget that type of thing . . .

'I'm telling you again, Laura, dare, take the step. I'm here for you. Where are you right now? At the station? Come to me. I'm waiting for you. We'll talk about us. And we'll talk about the show. I have some ideas. You'll like them.'

*

For Luc, a doctor friend, it's been going on for six years. 'One day I was giving a lecture in Bordeaux,' he tells me. 'The next morning at the hotel, the reception-ist tells me that a woman came and left a package for me. In it there was some foie gras and Château-Margaux . . . was she an admirer? I was flattered! In the basket there was a card. I didn't know the woman but I hurried to thank her, and I added to my note a copy of my latest book that had just been published . . . Big mistake! Just the fact that I responded . . . I have never been able to get rid of her!'

'What do you mean?'

'Since that day, she floods me with various pack-ages. Letters addressed to her, photos of her at her first communion, a statue of an elephant, notes she took at various lectures, flash drives. One day she sent me jew-ellery. And even her purse. An old purse made out of crocodile skin from the 1950s.'

'Is it still going on?'

'It never stops, I received another envelope yester-day . . . I don't open anything any more. I quickly rec-ognized her handwriting. But I got tired of going to the post office to return the packages to her. Now I have a box full of stuff in my office. I could show you, if you'd like to see it.'

'Does she still go to your lectures?'

'Wherever I go, she's there, in the first row. She stares at me—how can I put it?—with a lost look. As if she's suspended. The look of a dog that's waiting to be petted. Or waiting for a sign that it should hurry to me. It's really difficult. The slightest act is interpreted, milled, shaped into a form of acquiescence. If I happen to glance at her while I'm speaking, I know that I've reignited . . . I don't even know what . . . '

Luc thinks.

'What is striking, you see, is the absolute dissymmetry between people in this type of situation. On the one side there is that endless, limitless waiting. On the other, the opposite, a mixture of irritation, aggravation, concern . . . '

'Anxiety?'

'Anxiety, yes, about falling into the trap of compassion . . . At the beginning, it was hard. I tried reasoning with her. Because . . . I forgot to tell you but that woman is a physics prof—I wonder what this must look like in front of students! In short, she absolutely insisted that I direct her thesis. Of course, that was impossible. So I took the time to talk to her: "I can't, I have too many doctoral students now, I don't really understand your subject, etc." She took the blow, then started up again, even stronger. In her mind, I was constantly in denial. The denial of my own consent.'

'Then what happened?'

'Well . . . I stopped reasoning with her. I started acting distant and cold. I cut off all communication.'

'How did she react?'

'With silence. She didn't speak. I said to her, "I don't want to oversee your work, I don't want to read what you write, I don't want to receive things from you. I want you to stop, leave me alone. Forget me, you understand? Forget me!" She was quiet. God only knows what was going through her head during that silence. I sometimes wondered if she was going to pull a knife out of her purse.'

. . .

'We are in the realm of the unpredictable. The only thing I know is that every week I receive a letter from her. Often she brings it herself and leaves it with my secretary. She's there in person, she wanders the halls of the university. It's a very destabilizing situation. You control neither the beginning nor the end. You don't know where it comes from, what triggered it, and how it might end. You don't know what kind of fantasy you might be the object of. And you are completely outside the rational world in which you've existed since childhood . . .'

I look at Luc without saying anything. He emphasizes the powerlessness that is driving him crazy.

'Nothing,' he says, 'nothing that passes through words is effective. Anything I might say, anything anyone else might say, has no effect. But it goes even further. The slightest non-verbal communication—a movement, a look, blinking your eyes—reactivates the delusion. So when you are in such an impasse something primitive takes hold of you. A visceral aggression. The rage that floods you when the failure of language no longer leaves any other option than that of violence. Of lashing out.'

Luc frowns a bit.

'No, I assure you, you should come see what she's sent me. It does have its funny aspects. One day I received a cheque that of course I didn't cash. Also the keys to her apartment with a note: "When are you coming?" But now, your turn, Laura. Tell me about your novel. Who is this C?'

*

Who is this C? Who is this C whose full name I never write? An American friend I told about my novel and C started calling her 'The Creepy Woman'. 'C for de Clérambault'. 'C for Creepy'. That's it exactly. I realize I can't even say her name any more. That it makes me sick to do it. As if uttering her name would enhance that mild panic Riccardo spoke about. When I think that her first name evokes transparency and clarity! What irony! At the station there is another C in my department. Each time a colleague mentions her I shudder. I have the feeling that this first name carries a dark portent. By using only the first letter I stay at a distance. I handle the bad spirit with tweezers.

*

That doesn't prevent C from being an overwhelming presence. What strikes me is the symmetry that has settled in what she calls 'our relationship'. C is obsessed with me and she is obsessing me, in turn. Her presence has grown like a gas that expands and is smothering me from the inside. I'm suffocating. I'm exhausted.

*

An email from C:

'Laura, are you there? I can see you're in your office . . . '

An email from C:

'Laura, why won't you answer me? Laura . . . '

*

Enough! I open another mailbox. A virgin space that has not been polluted by C.

bebita@gmail.com is the secret address that Eduardo created for me. He's the only one who uses it. To make me laugh or to tell me that he loves me, which is certainly the same thing.

'Hola, Bebita . . .' Then there are a few 'Mexicomic' messages. Eduardo explains that that's what he calls them since he read a 'Mexicomedy' by Carlos Fuentes in the airplane. Apart from that, he's working like a dog all day long, which in his language means that he's working like crazy, and he sends sacks of *besos* to his *gringa*.

'P.S. Do you know where the word *gringo* comes from? In 1846 there was the war between the United States and Mexico. The Americans went off to war singing "Green Grows the Grass" and the Mexicans thought they were saying "Gringos, the Grass". And speaking of grass—which, as you know, is always greener on the other side—remind me to tell you about Tezcatlipoca. It's for your show . . . I know, you're going to tell me it's another unpronounceable name that doesn't work on TV. But he's the brother of good old Quetzalcoatl of the Aztecs. Well, Tezcatlipoca was so jealous of Quetzalcoatl that, if you're good, I'll tell you what type of diabolical trick he came up with to get him off the throne, shatter his reputation, steal his fiancée, and be Quetzalcoatl in Quetzalcoatl's place. In fact, Tezcatlipoca, in Aztecan, means "smoking mirror".'

*

At home I think of Eduardo. Only three more days until he gets home.

Stuck on the fridge is one of those little papers he collects. Who knows where he finds them. At the exit of the Métro. And he has fun sticking them onto the fridge.

'Monsieur Elhadj, super clairvoyant. Guaranteed [sic] results in a set amount of time. Resolve the most desperate of problems and ensure your future. Neutralize all adversaries and harmful or evil influences. Overcome and defeat any obstacle. So no one takes your beloved from you [sic]. The man or woman who has left, come here, you will see him/her! If you want immediate results, come right away!'

Next to that, Mr Djibril promises the same thing: 'Removal of spells, absolute protection against enemies. Your life will be transformed.' Mr Djibril proposes a 'serious, fast, and multipurpose work'. He promises to succeed 'where others have failed' and offers 'flexible payment plans'.

Am I under a spell? Should I consult one of the authorities on the fridge? Mr Djibril or Mr Elhadj who only see people by appointment from '10 a.m.–10 p.m. at 20 rue du Maroc, Paris 19e, Métro Gambetta'. The idea makes me smile . . . If they only knew. Me, the 'square' girl. The queen of calm and cool judgement— at least, that's how they see me at the station . . . Here I am on the verge of consulting the neighbourhood seer!

*

No, no, no, it's PH I will go to see again tomorrow. But PH . . . How can I put it? I was brimming with enthusiasm when I first went to see him. 'I'm dressed as you' and what followed . . . I wanted him to help me write a novel . . . Now that things have taken on other proportions . . . I realize I'm alone. That I'm not doing so well. In Eduardo's absence, could PH help me?

*

Email from C:
    'Answer me, please.'

*

I'm cold. I make some tea. Sitting at the kitchen table, staring at nothing, shivering, I wrap my hands around the cup and hold the cup under my chin. On the fridge there is also a detail from a painting by Frida Kahlo. She has a hole in her forehead, and through the hole one can see inside her skull. That's what I wanted to do. Look inside C's head. Drill a very circular hole, like a disk, and look into it. *E pericoloso sporgersi.* At the bottom of the hole in Kahlo, there is a small, green landscape. With the head of a dead person in the centre.

*

Tucked up in my sheets, I continue reading. I no longer see things very clearly.

*

Around 1930, de Clérambault doesn't see very clearly, either. He is losing his sight. Double cataracts. He can't work any more. Feels dependent, discouraged.

He decides to go to Barcelona where he has heard about Dr Ignacio Barraquer, a pillar of the international ophthalmology community who has perfected a revolutionary method for removing the crystalline growths. But the operation is a failure. De Clérambault will never again see the world as he did before. In his biography of the doctor, Alain Rubens writes that he henceforth saw only strange geometric figures. 'The right eye has a tendency to see diamonds, whereas the left sees squares . . . One is tempted to wonder if de Clérambault isn't living in a both cubist and impressionist painting.'

*

I, too, have the impression that I'm living in deformed reality. And which is deforming me, in turn. Because of this situation I'm no longer the same. This is what I have to explain to PH. That C's obsession has brought on another, my own, exactly symmetrical. That it has created its double, like in a mirror. That my mind is besieged by her presence as if by a dybbuk. When I close my eyes she's there, stuck under my eyelids. Making my crystals opaque.

*

Emails from C. Four messages follow one another in rapid succession. I sense some bitterness, for the first time. She's going out of her way for me. She wants to help me flourish, become who I am, to be fully myself, without anxiety, happy. She only wants—has ever only wanted—my well-being. And I don't even have the decency to respond!

*

C is blurring my vision of things, contaminating my thoughts, paralysing me. Physically. At the station I try to avoid her. But, this morning, she caught me by surprise. I was waiting for the lift on the ground floor when I felt a presence behind me. Someone must have approached close enough to provoke imperceptible sensorial variations in my personal space. As if, without the slightest physical contact, my body had the intuition that another body was there, just behind it. Too close. Much too close . . .

Out of instinct I turned around. C was so close that I jumped. I didn't expect to be nose-to-nose or, rather, face-to-face with her. I saw a dark light in her eyes.

*

While thinking of that scene again later, I'm mad at myself for showing I was upset. Instead of pretending to be relaxed and getting into the lift when it arrived,

I stayed glued to the ground. Changed by Medusa into an immovable rock. The doors opened. I saw a polished shoe move towards them. C got in, erect, without a word. Smiling a smile that seemed hostile. As for me, I couldn't take a step. Or walk away. Or take out my phone to appear nonchalant. I was like a startled cat, all the hair sticking up, electrified by a halo of negative waves. And I stayed there, petrified, while the doors closed on her sinister smile.

4

Am I the One Going Crazy?

In the hallways of the television station, I now turn around all the time to see if C is following me. I'm more afraid than ever that she's watching me, that she'll send me more messages on my phone or my computer, that I'll run into her in the cafeteria, in the ladies room . . . I hate seeing her go by, even at a distance, standing straight as an arrow on her stiletto heels. I make up any excuse I can to avoid the meetings I know she'll be attending.

*

I think about Dr M. I have questions that I should have asked him for my novel. Just as pheromones can 'fly' around two people in love, are there comparable chemical substances in mammals that can explain detestation, suspicion, hatred? Do molecules that act as messengers between two beings transmit information to our brains and play a role in our social behaviour—attraction, repulsion, aggression, sexuality?

During the 'lift scene', I seemed to have detected something threatening around C. Particles of hostility. They had triggered infinitesimal signals that I had perceived like a reptile or an insect might do. What portion of our animal nature might be playing in our story?

*

After the scene in the lift, since it is now impossible to concentrate, I gather my things and leave the office. My idea is to hole up in the Café des Arts. One part of me says to the other, 'You'll be able to work more efficiently there.' In reality, I already know that I won't get anything done—at least nothing constructive for my programme. I feel guilty, but it is stronger than I. I take out a book that Dr M had given me, *Consciousness, the Brain, States of Awareness, and Alternate Realities*.

'Here,' he said as I was getting ready to leave.

We had spoken of obsessive disorders, compulsion, and I was about to ask him how to scientifically explain that C's obsession was obsessing me to the point that I was ending up obsessing over the idea that her obsession was obsessing me! I remembered his answer and I had even more questions. Had a loop also started up in my brain? Could C's grey matter communicate with mine without my consent? How was it that someone who wasn't ill could—a bit like in the case of passive smoking—catch by mere contact the same madness as another?

'I'm the prisoner of the brain of another,' I had almost told him. 'I'm afraid of what that brain might do to mine.'

Seeming to read my mind—but maybe he really wanted to change the subject—Dr M had given me a book whose enigmatic cover had two blue eyes on either side of a staircase.

'Here . . . You, who seem to be dreaming that we can reconcile psychology, the neurosciences and literature . . . ' at that moment it seemed that an ironic smile was forming on his face—'you have to read this. I'm sure that, even for a literary person like you these pages will inspire interesting reflections on the way in which we perceive the world and ourselves. Now, my dear madame . . . excuse me . . . the staff . . . ' he had said while looking at the time on the phone he had just taken out of his hip pocket.

*

I put my phone on silent mode. Again, another message from C:

'I've thought about it, Laura. Not only are you incapable of seeing what is good, generous and loving in my messages. But the fact that you don't even bother responding is unforgivable. You always thought you were more intelligent, didn't you? Superior . . . say something, at least . . . '

*

In the diagrams in the book Dr M gave me, I find the well-known basal ganglia. They are there, nice and warm, at the heart of the brain and its thirty billion neurons. Stylized as if I, myself, had drawn one of those sheep brains that I can still see, laid out in C's father's butcher shop, and which always disgusted me. The caption explains that above the cerebellum there are three important appendices, the basal ganglia and the cortex, which regulate movement, as well as the hippocampus, necessary for memory. With, also above, the brainstem, the most ancient element from an evolutionary point of view.

*

The enlarged view of a synapse, with, highlighted, the synaptic vesicles and neurotransmitters, makes me think of a painting by Klimt, something aquatic where the long arms of dendrites float nonchalantly like algae. I'm having trouble making the connection between these descriptions and C's problem. Is this all we are? A thinking network of axons? A tangling of neurons? A chemistry of neurotransmitters that govern *in fine* all our behaviour? I tell myself that if that is the case, writing a novel seems impossible. Who are we if we're not ourselves? Is C not herself or is she not what I believed that she had always been?

My head is in my hands. The waitress at the Café des Arts, the blond woman I like, approaches me, concerned: 'Are you OK? . . . '

'Yes, I'm fine . . . ' I answer, sitting up.

*

An email from C:

'Still no word from you. You're disrespecting me, that's obvious. Let me remind you that you're the one who started this. You're the one who made me understand that you love me. Twice. That gives you a responsibility, Laura. Whether you like it or not, you have a responsibility towards me . . .'

*

A responsibility. That word really hits home. Responsibilities, duties, injunctions, aggression. All of a sudden, I see nothing but that all around me. I'm living in a world in which everything, animate and inanimate objects, are giving me orders. There are obvious instructions, the phone telling me 'wake up' in the morning, the snooze button, the radio 'listen to me', the clock 'hurry up', the fridge 'fill me', the almost spoiled food 'eat me', the flat 'clean me', the bills 'pay me', the ads 'buy me', the beggar in the street 'give me' . . . To which all sorts of other messages are added—open me, write to me, answer me, comment on me, explain to me, like me . . . The phone—answer me, speak to me, remind me, listen to me, comfort me, complain to me . . . The TV (through my programme)—interest me, amuse me, captivate me, distract me, surprise me, hook me . . .

Even before C I was already suffering from this 'imperative' world. I saw myself, like Saint Sebastian, pierced by an additional arrow each time something came demanding my attention. And now a madwoman was claiming that I had a responsibility towards her. Was giving me and repeating over and over the supreme order: Love me! Be me!

*

On rue Soufflot, PH must sense that I'm not doing very well. He repeats that I should have run away. 'This novel you're writing,' he says, shaking his head . . .

'What do you mean, this novel?'

He passes his finger over his moustache. 'You want to understand, but you're getting too close, Laura . . . you're giving assurances . . . '

'???'

'With de Clérambault patients, I've told you a thousand times—it's dangerous. Your C is clearly wily and intelligent, but she's very ill. Cut all ties. Flee. Believe me, in your case, there is nothing else to be done.'

*

PH is nice, but I need my work. 'I need it,' I tell him, looking into his eyes. 'There's no other station that airs the kind of programme I do. And I fought to be able to work in this media. I love it. I've proven myself. I was doing so well until something started malfunctioning in the brain of someone else . . . Flee? But how?'

*

I asked PH how much time de Clérambault Syndrome 'usually' lasted. 'Well,' he responded, 'as far as Alexia is concerned, she told you, Bruel has loved her for almost twenty years. But I know of cases that have gone on for much longer. When we met the first time, you remember, I mentioned a patient who was fixated on Johnny Hallyday. In fact, it was a real patient of mine. Johnny has been giving her signs for more than thirty years. And she ended up going out with one of his look-alikes. Which didn't cure her—by the way, it's a guy who is reaping the rewards by getting money from her for drugs . . . Anyway, going back to that woman, it all began when she was twenty and was a Johnny groupie. Now she's fifty and is completely messed up, destroyed by alcohol. And yet I can assure you that there is something in her as fresh as the first day. It's Johnny's voice that has settled up there—' PH touches his temple with his left index finger. 'It is there, in the cockpit, and it never stops singing.'

*

'What will happen?' I ask PH. 'What would happen if Johnny arrived today and said to the patient, "OK, I was wrong. You were right. I've loved you since the first concert, but I never wanted to admit it to myself"?' PH seems to think my question is absurd, but he doesn't say so. 'If Johnny took her in his arms, just like that? Well . . . that would immediately provoke a passing to the act or a hyperdelusional episode,' he said. 'She would kill him, I think. "You understand, Doctor . . . Someone was pretending to be Johnny and wanted to . . . I had to kill him."'

PH rubs his moustache, looks in the distance. Then concludes, 'That's it, yes . . . She would kill him, or would kill herself. There is no cure for eroto-maniacs. No solution to the delusion.'

*

An endless love.

5

Love, to Really Make Someone Suffer

From all the time I've been spending thinking of de Clérambault, doing research, making notes, I suddenly become aware of how far behind I've got on my programme. I really need to prepare for my show. I still don't have a guest. A guest I no longer have a lot of time to find. I wonder how I've managed all these years to pull off the show so lightly. Everything seems so heavy, so complicated now. I really must start concentrating on it.

*

De Clérambault. I think about all the different stages PH described. Following the ardent exaltation, there is disappointment, bitterness. And yet, from the outside, nothing can be seen. The more I flounder at the office, the more C, on the contrary, appears normal and at ease. She's even doing better and better. Often smiling, laughing out loud. This must be her strategy. So that no one at the station has yet to notice anything.

Recently she spontaneously said—but I sensed it
was targeted at me—'You should laugh at least once a
day. It's good for your health.' The funnier and more
extroverted she seems, the more I appear serious and
introverted.

*

One day she is particularly upbeat. Even with me,
which is bizarre. I can't figure out what is going on.
Suddenly she bursts into my office and tells me that
she wants us to work together on my show. A lead
cloak drops on my shoulders. I try to find the most
neutral words I can. I respond that it isn't possible.
She's sitting at the meeting table, right behind the one
where I'm working. Sticks out her legs, and crosses her
crocodile pumps on the back of another chair.

Don't turn around. Don't look at her. I stare obsti-
nately at my computer but sense her presence at my
back. The waves again . . . Concentric like circles in the
water. Growing and reaching me. I hear her say that we
are going to work arm in arm. That the theme of jealousy has always enthralled her. That it's a wonderful
project.

*

I don't say a word. She continues. She wants to show me that she has ideas. 'We can't use too much Proust,' she says. 'There are so many jealous characters in *Remembrance of Things Past* . . . Saint-Loup, Gilberte, and of course, Swann, because of the beautiful Odette. You remember how Proust defined jealousy: "The shadow of love." Its "lamentable and contradictory growth . . . " It's great, isn't it? OK, of course, you have to go back to the original story. Cain killing Abel. The primitive scene. That will be easier to illustrate, too. We can show Tintoretto on the screen. Obviously, you know that famous painting by Tintoretto?'

*

She says that the way she used to speak in the past: 'What? You've never seen *Blowup*? You don't know *The Music Lesson*? Come on, you really must read Pindar . . . ' I am about to explode. I make an enormous effort not to throw myself at her. Make her disappear from my office. Make her disappear for ever . . . But she calmly continues her presentation. She has clearly thought about it. And when she brings up Agrippina and Madame de Montespan, she says things that I recognize because . . . I wrote them myself.

*

How did C get into my computer? How did she find my password? (Eduardo, it's true, is not difficult to guess, but 80, two numbers that I used at random because you had to have two numbers after the letters?). I wonder if she has had copies of the keys to my office made. I imagine her going through drawers, trying on the dance shoes I keep in one of them for a class I take, or my red lipstick that I use for important interviews. My thoughts are wandering when I hear her complete the sentence: '. . . this will be a fantastic opportunity.'

*

What fantastic opportunity? I don't want to work with her. I don't want to. I don't want to. I can't stand her behind me in my office. I want her to disappear. That she . . . And in a voice that I would like to be as calm as possible, I tell her that the idea for this show is mine, and that I prefer to work on it alone.

*

I don't know if de Clérambault developed this theme. The simmering resentment of love. Or the opposite . . . Later, I learnt that C went to complain to the department head. I stole her ideas, I refuse to work with her, I'm impeding her progress, I think I'm superior, I have no sense of the 'group' . . . I'm speechless. I can see just how well, beyond her madness, C knows me. She knows what will certainly hurt me. There is knowledge behind her cruelty. You have to love someone to really make them suffer.

*

Hands, arms, shoulders: I am no longer anything but a living anthill. I think about an exhibition on ants that I saw a few months ago. In a video taken in South America, a certain species of ants organized themselves to set a trap for a butterfly. They lived on the stalk of a plant. They dug holes where they awaited their prey. When the butterfly settled, they sprayed it with their paralysing venom. The name of this ant suddenly came back to me. It was called *Gigantiops destructor*.

*

When I leave the editing room, an open space where editors, journalists, photojournalists, documentation specialists and assistants work, I can hear people whispering. When I leave my office and go into that room again, everyone is quiet. Everyone is busily typing on their computers.

*

Hostility, solitude, guilt. I must have done something to deserve all this.

6

Held Hostage by the Brain of Another

I had almost forgotten the false Facebook account. But now it comes back to me like a boomerang.

'What? You're going to have Trierweiler on your show on jealousy?' a friend asks me in an email.

Other messages follow to congratulate me.

'What a great idea! Trierweiler in person on your set. And to talk about jealousy. Spilling her guts . . . How did you manage to "get" her?'

'Finally, you're announcing your subjects on FB. It was about time . . . '

*

Consumed by a cold rage, I burst into C's office. It's been some time since I've set foot in there. That I've approached it by closer than ten metres.

'What the hell is all this?'

She looks at me with her icy stare and her forced smile.

'Do you realize? Do you have any idea what you've done?'

'Open your eyes, Laura, we're going to do great things together. To have that woman on the show is an amazing coup for our programme,' she says, glancing apparently nonchalantly at her shoes.

Our programme? I repeat that it's *my* programme, that I forbid her to be involved in it, I order her to shut down that account immediately, to stop pretending to be me and to forget me. Can she get that? For-get-me.

*

I must have shouted. She closes the door to her office—with one of her stilettos—and looks at me with a pitying look. Compassionate. Like the way a mother would look at her child during an adolescent temper tantrum. A look that means: 'You're disappointing me, and causing me pain . . . Are you making me suffer on purpose? I'm used to it. You're testing me—I still love you . . . It's a difficult stage, I know how you feel . . . I know what you're feeling, because I am you . . .'

*

Solitude, weight, vertigo. Still guilt.

I need to talk. I go to see Luc at the university. As he had suggested, I do an inventory of what his 'delusional' has recently sent him.

A black shirt.

Black stockings in a cellophane bag.

A cell phone.

A woman's shopping bag.

Two tubes of paint, one black and one white, in a brown paper envelope.

A set of keys—no doubt hers.

A datebook—without any doubt hers.

A pair of glasses in a case.

Green felt Christmas ornaments.

An assortment of stale cookies dating from 2011.

Letters in German dating from the First World War.

Show bills.

A crocodile skin purse from the 1950s.

A black plate decorated with plane tree leaves.

A metal lizard.

Peruvian dolls . . .

'And there you have only what I've received in the past two years,' Luc says. 'I've thrown things out now and then, this is only a small sampling . . . Oh, look at that . . . it's the best!' He takes a pair of black-and-white slippers with pompoms out of a red plastic bag. 'I found them one day in front of the door to my office. It made the secretaries howl with laughter . . . She is incredibly inventive, all the same . . . And everything has a meaning. Which I don't always catch, but here . . . "Come to my place, put on your slippers, your address is my house . . . "' He shows me a small card on which she has written Luc's name with, just below, her address in Bordeaux. 'It's a bit creepy . . . So there it is, you've seen it . . . And it's been going on for six years.'

Luc seems to reflect, then shrugs his shoulders. 'Since I refuse to let this woman come into my life, she *forces* me to share hers . . . '

*

Luc is done with his classes. We go to a cafe near his school for some coffee.

'Still, there's a funny side to it,' he says, talking about that odd mix of stuff. That statement reminds me of Alexia's parents. 'It isn't funny at all,' they had insisted. 'You laugh, but it's awful. The solitude of those sick people is immeasurable. The moments of despair, of solitude, of pain—I defy anyone to endure what she endures,' her mother had said.

*

My boss called a department meeting. Officially it was to bring everyone up to date on the coming programming. All journalists were expected to be there.

'And you, Laura, where are you on jealousy?'

I explain the angle and the main focus of the documentary being filmed. I give the calendar and detail the composition of the set for the debate that will follow. A historian, a psychoanalyst and a final guest who remains to be found.

'What do you mean, who remains to be found? What about Trierweiler?'

Gigantiops destructor. Thousands of billions of ants like needles that are being stuck in my hands, arms, legs. I can't even speak. I hear myself mumble, 'Tr . . . ?'

'Of course,' says the boss. 'C's idea is excellent. You'll host together. That won't be too much with guests of that calibre. It's going to blow the audience away. And we need that. It's perfect!'

Around the table, the others are nodding their agreement, half-servile, half-distracted. C is smiling.

The boss, in a hurry, gets ready to go on to the next item.

'Wait . . . really, wait . . . ' I say. 'Is this a joke?'

I can feel C is looking at me. My voice is strained. Now it's the boss' turn to seem surprised. 'What's the problem?'

'The problem is that . . . I told C . . . I don't understand. No, no, no. It's out of the question. I'm hosting. I'm hosting alone. And I DON'T WANT Trierweiler.'

Those who were nodding off wake up and are looking at me, stunned.

'Listen,' I say to the boss, forcing myself to look at him. 'I'll come to your office after the meeting.'

*

He doesn't understand at all, and I understand that he hasn't understood anything. I had got myself into a big jam, but what could I tell him? That C is harassing me? That she's persuaded that I love her? That she's sick? Does he know about de Clérambault Syndrome? Léa who chained herself to the gates at Buckingham Palace? I couldn't see myself launching into that sort of explanation.

Or confronting the humiliations that would have followed: 'You're old enough to settle your differences between you, aren't you?' 'Don't you think there are more important things going on?' And the final blow: 'You're the one who said she should be hired.'

*

And so I explain that inviting a celebrity isn't at all the concept of the show. That it is stupid and vulgar. That I am even surprised that a station like ours could go in that direction. I don't convince him. There is only the manner of interviewing that can be stupid or vulgar, he replies, in a tone that seems to say, 'You're such a snob.' Then he emphasizes the need for the show to 'evolve'. For a moment I think he is going to tell me that C will be taking it over, that she will be able to do something much more current, that she wants to do it, that she has 'out-of-the-box ideas'. I am trapped.

*

'I will never leave you.' At that moment I truly understand what that phrase meant. I will never leave you. I will never leave. It's the same thing. I will never be able to 'disengage' C. No de Clérambault–type predator will ever release its prey.

*

A bit earlier I had read an interview with Bruel in *Pariscope*. 'It's been six years since my previous album and *Lequel de nous*,' he said. With his films, theatre, his book, poker and his children, he did 'so many things' that, yes, it had taken him six years to finish this album that was being talked about today. I concluded from this that when I met Alexia, she recited to me by heart the words of a song that had not yet come out. How did she know of it? I read between the lines. Bruel was performing in New York and London. Did Alexia follow him? Would she have chained herself to the gates of Gramercy Park or Buckingham Palace like de Clérambault's Léa? Bruel explained that he was working on two new films. I tried to guess what signs Alexia might have seen in this. For one of them, *Tu veux ou tu veux pas?*, it wasn't difficult. For the other, *Les yeux jaunes des crocodiles*, it was harder. 'Bruelmania hasn't aged at all,' said the article. But Alexia had aged twenty years.

*

I remember asking Alexia's parents how it had all begun. I wanted their version. Alexia had seen Patrick Bruel after the concert and there had been that meeting of eyes. 'It was in a hall. *I'm* the one he looked at,' she told them euphorically. At the time, they paid little attention. 'There were three girls. Three friends who were crazy about him,' said her father. 'Remember?' he asked his wife, 'They called him Patri-i-i-i-i-i-ck. It was sweet. The other two got over it, but Alexia never did.'

*

What had been triggered? How had the 'loop' been created? I think about the flyer I had taken from Dr M's waiting room.

One person out of eight will one day be stricken with an illness of the brain or the spinal cord: Alzheimers, Parkinson's, stroke, ALS, MS, epilepsy, depression, panic attacks, schizophrenia, autism, OCD...

The flyer lists a certain number of neurological or psychiatric illnesses. What it doesn't say is how one can become crazy because one has found oneself overnight hostage to a deranged brain that is not one's own. *Gigantiops destructor.*

*

That's where I am in my thoughts when Pauline, a journalist who was at the meeting, comes into my office, apparently concerned. Wasn't I overdoing it a bit by shouting like that?

'Oh, yes, yes. You shouted, "No, no, no!"'

Hadn't I overreacted? Then, in a tone of confidence: Hasn't C been my friend up to then? Was I OK? I feel an invisible ceiling falling down, ready to crush me.

*

Get a hold of myself. I try to explain to myself—to better explain to her?—what in C's behaviour has caused me such anxiety. Luc perhaps put his finger on the heart of the problem—the idea of being expropriated, placed outside oneself. Thought of by others.

All my life I've believed in free will. Fought to be the master of my destiny. 'One is what one wants to be,' repeated my mother when I was young. That meant you are the only captain on board. And in the event of failure, there were no excuses. You hadn't tried hard enough, wanted badly enough. *Try harder . . .* I've always found it difficult to know exactly what I wanted. But now here was someone else who was starting to want for me. Someone else had irrupted into my life and was suddenly telling me: 'You are what I want.'

*

Sartre's marvellous phrase comes back to me: 'We are what we do with that which others wish to do with us.'

*

I never wanted to be the one that C wants me to be—the one who loves her and who doesn't want what's best for her. It is unbearable to be labelled like that in the eyes of the others. Fixed like an insect caught in resin. When we were children, one of my cousins made that sort of 'stop-action' that we never tired of observing. We saw flying things, flies or butterflies, stopped for ever in flight. Taken in full action, like the bodies in the lava of Pompeii. Death around life.

*

To be and to want. Was it really so simple, what I was discovering? That each one of us depended on others. Did a butterfly ever want to end up in resin?

*

There is more. C has emptied me of all that I had that was living, spontaneity, is filling me with a mixture of confusion, doubt, stress, a horrible feeling of isolation, and, in the end, a terrible fear of dying. Who am I? I feel I am crumbling. Nothing is holding any more. And how can I explain that around me? Every time I try to say something, that something seems hollow and ridiculous. Is even language losing its value?

*

'Well . . . ' Pauline continues, 'if you want, we can talk about it at the cocktail party later . . . '

Oh my God, the Press Club cocktail party! I've completely forgotten! What a mess!

I'm going to have to force myself. I could get in trouble for not being there.

*

On the way to the party that evening I think things over. Here I am 'alienated' (made another) by an 'alienated' (a madwoman such as they were called in the time of the 'alienist' de Clérambault). But by seeing her as a sick person, aren't I then labelling her, as well? She doesn't always behave the way I see her. Her delusion affects only me. And above all, if she is sick—de Clérambault indeed shows that pretending to be normal can be part of the pathology—so if she's sick, is she responsible? Is she what she wants? I feel myself entangled in a thousand questions. The most disconcerting, I tell myself, is that C is putting her 'illness' in the service of my 'wellness'. Are the sick innocent? Aren't they themselves?

*

Another doubt. In wanting to understand her pathology better, aren't I seeking to rid myself of any responsibility? To put in place an unconscious and useful strategy . . . because I don't want to see? To see what I, myself, have brought to life in C. That old wound from high school. That attraction that, I must admit, had come from me at the time . . . Is C right? Am I guilty?

*

At the Press Club cocktail party, I discover the roof terrace of the Molitor, that new Paris hotel that has just opened near the Bois de Boulogne. Even before entering the crowd, I see Pauline who is coming towards me, a plate in her hand.

'We can go over there,' she says. 'on the little terrace behind the bar. It's still under construction, but it will be quieter.'

At an angle that I hadn't seen, there is a space that is not yet completely constructed and that we reach by crossing a rather dangerous passageway. Why is she insisting that we find a quiet spot? So that C doesn't see us? I've always liked Pauline. Her easygoing nature. This evening she has slipped into the role of confidant that she is clearly taking seriously. C has spoken to her. As well as to the whole team. She has presented things in such a way that she is the victim and I am the bully.

'She isn't sleeping at night,' Pauline tells me. 'She sees that you're avoiding her, and it really hurts her. Why did you refuse to work with her on the show?'

Pauline continues. C feels excluded. She's suffering. Am I aware that I'm causing her to suffer? Then she repeats, 'Weren't you friends before?' As if a broken friendship disturbed her more than if I had told her that I was leaving Eduardo.

When she asks me to talk about C, I'm forced to remain positive. C has obviously told the worst things about me. To say nothing would pique her curiosity. Explain that C is in love with me? To love is not a sin. Reveal that she is sick? When at the office she behaves in a completely normal way?

*

I'm feeling worse and worse. I'm careful of anything I might say. I'm afraid that this conversation will end up turning against me. Will reveal how disgusted I am now with C. I'm horrified at my distrust. I think of H, an old friend who, citing Stendhal, said that one cannot spend one's life hating and being afraid. I detest the fact that C is forcing me to hate her. I detest the fact that she is forcing me to be afraid.

*

Until that woman had reappeared in my life, I thought I had made some progress. But all my old fears have come back. I had got rid of nothing. I also thought I had accomplished internal work that allowed me—at least I was naive enough to believe it—to be above intrigues, traps, manipulations . . . But C is sucking me down into something low. Forcing me to slog though it. If I defend myself, I will enter into the lowliness that I deplore. If I don't defend myself—which I have a tendency not to do through idiotic pride—my position becomes increasingly precarious. In both cases, I hate myself.

*

I am transfixed by these thoughts when a saving hand takes my arm. 'You can't stay here, ladies,' says a hotel employee, 'there's a problem with the guardrail on this part of the terrace. A malfunction. We're waiting on the experts, but you know how that is. If there's an issue with the contractor, it can take months . . . You'll have to go around the other way to get back to the little terrace.' I raise my glass, and without further ado, say to Pauline, 'Sorry, I have to leave. See you later!'

*

I return home unhappy and frustrated. What have I done to deserve such punishment? Prévert said that one mustn't allow intellectuals to play with matches. For the pleasure of writing, I got close to C. Too close to her flame. I didn't 'light' her, but I played with her. High bet, odd, low bet—nothing's working any more.

*

Think of something else. I must think of something else . . . Someone gave me the movie *Johnny Guitar*. I'm not keen on this film. I don't like Westerns. But this time I'm enthralled.

Hatred, the visceral hatred of a woman for another. Vienna, the sublime Joan Crawford, has purchased some land in a remote region of the United States over which a certain Emma reigns. Emma has everything, land and livestock for five hundred square miles. It doesn't matter. She can't stand Vienna's presence. Or her beauty, her success, the way the men like her . . .

In the past, Emma *was* Vienna. The one who ruled as the head woman. I'm Vienna, she might say. In fact, she doesn't say that. She only says, at the beginning of the film, 'I'm going to kill you.' At least in Westerns, things are clear.

I'm mesmerized. I stop at images, rewind. I try to see what Emma does to gradually convince the sheriff and his crew to join her murderous plan. Manipulation, seduction, intimidation. Emma plays on their virile pride. 'Look at her,' she says, speaking of Vienna. 'Standing up there . . . staring down on us . . . like a somebody.' She talks to those men like a hunter to his pack. 'Go get her! Drag her down!' and that 'Drag her down!' means 'Pull her off her pedestal!' 'Quarter her!' 'Rip her to pieces!' I think of C talking about me to the station staff. 'She despises us. It's a class thing . . . '

There is always a strategy among the perverse. Emma tries to implicate Vienna in the assassination of her brother. Vienna supposedly ordered it, and 'The Dancing Kid' supposedly carried it out. The Dancing Kid Emma is in love with. But she reverses things. She says, 'He was always eyeing me.' Listening to her, it was he who was constantly watching her, who loved her. Well, well. I'm ashamed to love you, so I imagine that you love me . . .

What about Emma? Obviously a victim. Who wants to see Vienna hanged with the Kid. 'I won't sleep till I see both of you hanged.'

I re-watch that incredible scene when Emma says these simple words: 'I'm going to kill you.' In the midst of her destructive fury, a smile forms on her lips. She has changed her tone, her pace. It's the only moment in the film when a true sweetness emanates from her.

It seems that Godard and Truffaut adored *Johnny Guitar*. The final scene is spectacular. The two women, each with her pistol, on either side of the house. Each determined to save her skin. Perfect symmetry . . . And Johnny watching . . .

I think of Eduardo. I see him with guns blazing, galloping to my rescue. The whole story now suddenly seems like an old colourized Western. C or me?

7
The Eduardo Disappointment

I don't know how many times I check the Internet to see if flight AF439 from Mexico has arrived. When the plane has finally landed, I leave the office without a word. At home, I scarcely have time to put the key in the lock when the door opens on Eduardo and his wonderful smile. There is something honest and calming in that face. A light that responds perfectly to what I need. At that moment I want to give Eduardo a shot of de Clérambault so he will also love me for ever and never leave me.

'¡Hola, Bebita!'

I cling to him! Something warm and animal-like. The door is still open, but we stay like that for several minutes.

'How did you get home from the airport so quickly?'

He has a knowing expression, closes the door with his foot, takes off my coat and puts his hand under my blouse.

'Your breasts are soft, my Bebita.'

'Eduardo . . . '

'Your body is luscious,' he says, leading me to the living room.

'Luscious?'

'That means silky, perfumed, liquid . . . '

My shoes fall off on the floor. After we make love we stay lying together for a long time. I'd like to erase the past few days like a magic screen.

'Eduardo?'

'Hmmm?'

' . . . I'm afraid . . . '

'That's good.'

'What do you mean?'

'Just that, Bebita. Simply that. It's good to be afraid. You must always be a little afraid, it's very reassuring. The people who aren't afraid have always been disturbing to me. Even dangerous. Don't you agree?'

What I like about Eduardo, apart from his accent, is his unstoppable will to make me laugh. This time, however, I want to make him understand that it's something else.

'I'm not joking, Eduardo . . . '

'Do I look like I'm joking, Bebita? I couldn't be more serious.'

He hugs me tighter, shaking me a bit. Then he continues, softer, as if he is whispering a secret:

'Since I've known you you've always been afraid of something. Afraid of not succeeding, afraid of not being up to the task, afraid of crumbling under the weight of it all . . . It's because of that, Bebita . . . because of that that you are beautiful and you do what you do. If you weren't afraid, you wouldn't be anything. ¿Entiendes?'

'Eduardo, something's happened.'

'Something's happened?'

'C. The woman who works with me . . . you remember? I think she's in love with me.'

Eduardo bursts out laughing.

'She loves you? I can understand that. I love you, too . . . '

'No, Eduardo, don't say you understand. I assure you that you don't understand.'

I tell him about the harassment, the telephone calls during the night, about everything PH explained, my own research on de Clérambault.

'Well, she's lucky to be persuaded that you love her, because I will ask myself that until the day I die. I'm the anti–de Clérambault, if I've understood this. I have doubts, she has certainty. We should create the middle ground . . . '

Eduardo is in form. One would never guess that he has just travelled ten hours in a plane. I tell him how C 'dressed as me'. But when he answers that I should think about shopping at the great fashion houses, those that make unique clothing for unique women, I give up.

In the kitchen he pours a glass of Bordeaux. We drink together.

'Did you see a film during your flight?'

*

Let him breathe. Don't bombard him with my anxiety . . . A few days later, fate smiles on me. Eduardo and I are having dinner at the home of some old friends. There is a film producer, a banker and a therapist, an expert in psycho-trauma. She says she has just written a book on bullying. I'm startled. While Eduardo pours her some wine she says to the group, 'We often speak of the victims, but what do we know about the ones who are causing the suffering?' She specifies that she's talking within the framework of schools. I'm a little disappointed. I would have preferred that she teach me something about the behaviour of adult bullies. But are they really so different?

'When I call the parents to the school and explain to them that their child is bullying another child, they are always in denial,' she says. '"My child a bully? Never!"' Still holding her glass out to Eduardo, she says that this process is triggered at a very young age, that it ends up in adolescence, and that it is then pursued over social networks. 'Anonymous, the subject is even less inhibited,' she says. 'These days, as you no doubt know, cyber-bullying has become a serious problem.'

*

Later, when coffee is served, I ask her what her 'patients' are like. She describes them as young people who take care of themselves, their appearance, surrounded by friends. Self-assured, and who seem very at ease with themselves. I think of C, so apparently at ease and charming. But the therapist speaks of an 'identity break'. Of weak self-esteem that explains their need to assert themselves by being aggressive towards others. 'What is striking is that they have neither rules nor limits. No awareness of the harm they are causing. No sense of guilt. When they speak of a victim they say, "She was asking for it." From the point of view of psychopathology, those are the most disturbing.'

*

We get home late that evening. Yet I can't help talking to Eduardo about C. Once again, he jokes. I try to remember who defined humour as humanity's best friend. I've always liked Eduardo's. But this time, I need him to be serious. Can't he make an effort?

'If I follow you, this woman is possessed by you and you're ending up being possessed by her?'

'Well, that's sort of right . . . ' I say, telling him about de Clérambault and the syndrome again.

He seems to be thinking about it.

'You know, in my grandmother's village in Chiapas, people really believe that. Being under a spell, the syndrome of influence. Someone who is introduced into your body and takes you over from yourself.'

'No, Eduardo . . . '

'Aztec healers, that is, those who descended from them, use a powder, a mixture of herbs and resin. In any case, that's what my grandmother explained to me one day . . . *Abuela querida*. It was a long time ago . . . What a pity that I didn't have time to go to Chiapas.'

Eduardo moves his arms around and describes that 'domination powder' which, according to the traditions of his ancestors, enable the elimination of a rival or to take control of a situation.

I can see that he doesn't believe in it for a minute, but he doesn't mind the stories. His voice always becomes tender when he tells about the pre-Columbian heritage of his compatriots. The way the old superstitions infiltrate daily life, even today.

'Eduardo . . . '

'It goes a long way, you know,' he says, interrupting, and throwing his jacket on the armchair in our bedroom. And while he is untying his tie, to my great stupefaction, he launches into stories of qualifications for the last World Cup soccer tournament.

'Imagine that a Mexican newspaper has surfed on this wave and explained to its readers how to cast a spell on the gringo team . . . '

I look at him, stunned. He knows I know nothing about soccer. That I detest it.

'Well, Bebita, believe it or not, it worked so well that they did it again for the matches against Honduras, Costa Rica and El Salvador. Sometimes I tell myself that the French team might learn something.'

He chuckles, then continues, 'I should bring you to Abuela's village. Abuela believes in all of that. She even speaks a bit of Nahuatl, the language of the ancient Aztecs. It's a very beautiful language, you know. Maybe

one of the most beautiful in the world with its allitera-
tions and its singing cadence . . . When I was little, I
must have been eight or nine, she took me to the
Museum of Anthropology. The one in Chapultepec we
visited a few times. You remember that wooden statue?
A woman with her hair braided and piled on top of her
head that inspired Frida Kahlo for one of her portraits?
Well, Abuela explained to me that that woman was . . .
wait, it's coming to me . . . the goddess of I can't remember what but who was connected to those beliefs.
In possession . . . I'm going to remember . . . no, I
can't. What I do remember, though, is that one day
Abuela wanted me to attend a ritual. I can still hear her
explaining what you had to do to get rid of a demonic
presence: "You burn a red candle, you rub the powder
in your hands above the flame. And you concentrate
your negative thoughts on your adversary . . . "'

*

Fine powder. An image flies through my mind. That of
my mother's little office with the shelves of pharmacy
jars all lined up. Jars containing powders, roots and
dried leaves. Jars of blue glass with slightly scuffed
green metal tops and a gold label with the most poetic
names. Black iron oxide, shavings of pomegranate
roots, maidenhair fern, red cinchona-bark powder,

light magnesium hydroxide, tincture of sundews . . .
suddenly I see a jar that is smaller than the others.
'Powder C: Belladonna'. It is surrounded with a red
strip with this word in capital letters printed on it:
TOXIC.

*

Eduardo is now stretched out on our bed, naked. He
holds out his arms to me. I'm mad that he didn't want
to listen to me. I shake my head—it's late.

'As you wish, Bebita. But at least come and hug me.
Like that? With your leg . . . '

He puts my leg on top of his. We hold hands. In
our secret language we call that 'closing the padlock'.

*

On the floor, next to me, on the ground. It's two-thirty
when the phone rings. I instinctively know it's not
the station. Or a subject that needs to be prepared
urgently. Or a 'great death' as we say in our journalism
jargon. But why in the world didn't I put the thing on
silent mode?

Too late. Eduardo is awake.

'What's going on? ¿Quién es?' he says angrily.

'You see? This is it . . . this is what I've been putting up with almost every night when you were away. And it never stops. This is exactly what I was trying to tell you. It's crazy . . . '

I didn't have time to continue. Eduardo, furious, turns on the little red lamp on the nightstand. Now he's pulling on the well-tucked sheet that doesn't want to move.

'What are you doing?'

'Listen, Bebita, I've been home for three days and that's all you've been talking about. This syndrome of who knows what . . . You don't realize it but it's getting on my nerves. Stop it. Take a breath, step back.'

This time I'm the one who gets angry. Which one of us doesn't realize? I raise my voice.

'OK,' I say, pounding my fist on the pillow. 'Can you listen to me for two minutes, without making fun of everything I say? Without joking about the Aztec rituals or avoiding the subject in one way or another?'

Eduardo is quiet and I start from the beginning. I tell about the station, the meeting, the perversion of the woman who went so far as to dig up Valérie Trierweiler to weasel her way into my show. I have trouble describing the pall that has come over me in the past few days. The impression that my show is threatened. The impression above all of being trapped, myself.

'I'm trapped, Eduardo. I've never gone through something like this. And I don't know what to do.'

*

I can see that he's making an effort. He is sitting on the edge of the bed and seems to be thinking. He tries to come up with a rational response, even if the entire story—indeed, because it isn't rational, at least on the surface—is beyond him, and makes him uncomfortable.

'Has she made any threats?'

I tell him that C is too savvy for that. That outside her love emails, nothing from her is ever written down. That she doesn't act directly. That I don't have anything that is sufficiently tangible.

'Not a word, not a threatening letter, something to convict? Someone who could testify for you . . . ? Do you want me to talk to my lawyer about it?'

Eduardo has his head in his hands. I see his wide, coppery back on the other side of the bed. I see his fingers running through his thick hair. So black. His clinched fingers that show his irritation.

'That would be great . . . '

'But . . . ?'

'But . . . ?'

When he turns around his face has softened.

'Are you sure that . . . what if she just wants to help you? Isn't she already helping you? I can see that it's annoying you but she is still providing you a great guest. It might not be such a bad idea, in fact. Don't be so stubborn, Bebita. Think. Maybe you should see her again. Have a cup of tea. Pop the abscess!'

I can see that Eduardo hasn't understood a thing. But I see him smile, probably satisfied that he found soothing words.

'You know, I'm still going to sleep in the living room,' he says, no longer pulling on the sheet. 'I have a very early conference call tomorrow. We'll both sleep better . . . Buenas noches, Bebita.'

*

I'm falling. A large inner wall has just crumbled. I can't accept that my problem is not also Eduardo's primary concern. I try again. We fight. It's the first time we've fought so hard. The first time I can't explain myself to him.

*

Insomnia. I think of my first meeting with PH. He had described the phases of the syndrome. I sum them up in my mind to understand better.

Exaltation. This is the moment of revelation. The subject suddenly becomes certain that the object secretly loves him. That it is he—the object—that first made advances, but that he doesn't dare or can't declare himself. From that there is what de Clérambault calls ardent expectation. A phase of insane hope during which the patient hopes that the beloved will finally declare himself openly.

Irritation. The patient understands that the object isn't 'responding'. Probably CAN'T respond. Because those around him—George V's court, Johnny's bodyguards—prevent it. A plot has been hatched against their happiness.

Bitterness. If the object doesn't respond it is probably because he doesn't WANT to respond. And what if it were he, the object, who is making fun of me? The patient wonders. He made me believe he was in love. He is playing with my feelings. He is manipulating me. He's an arsehole.

Passing to action.

*

But what exactly does that mean, passing to action? I realize that I never really discussed that with PH. 'Either they destroy themselves—they can, for example, commit suicide in front of the beloved—or they destroy the object,' he told me simply. He had added that to destroy could take all sorts of refined forms. 'In de Clérambault's time, for example, it was common to throw a bottle of sulphuric acid in the victim's face. It was very popular until the beginning of the twentieth century...'

*

Where was I when he told me that? I must have been thinking of the novel I was thinking of writing. I had found that literary descent.

*

Still can't sleep. IDEA—an idea that goes round and round while advancing. A strange idea that becomes an *idée fixe*, then a dark idea.

*

Actually, I have also gone through similar stages. Exaltation at the moment of discovering the syndrome (the story of Léa fascinated me, just as did the idea of writing a book on de Clérambault). Obsession (by being obsessed with me, C was able to haunt me in turn). Destruction (work, the couple—she is destroying everything. Even the way I look at myself has changed. Everything has become denatured).

A woman who is dressing as me has upended my world in an irreversible way.

8

Just a Nightmare

At the TV station, the air is thick. Viscous. As if something has happened. Pauline spills the beans. We're in the cafeteria and she has changed her role. From a confidant, she is now a judge. 'You're losing it, Laura,' she tells me, tapping the end of her cigarette on the table. 'Really, I . . . I don't get it . . .'

'But . . . I don't understand either. What's going on?'

She rolls her eyes.

'What's going on? Do you think such things aren't found out right away?'

'What in the world are you talking about?'

'Facebook, of course . . . about those unacceptable things you wrote to her. Just because she tried to help you with your show . . . No, Laura, really, you just can't do something like that. Even as a joke. You've gone way off base . . .'

My God, is she going to tell me, or keep staring at me? I repeat that I don't understand. I must look flabbergasted. Not only has the tingling started up again—I can feel my hands shaking around my tea cup—but I'm suddenly having trouble breathing. Meanwhile, Pauline continues to talk in a tone of someone who knows what's going on.

'I'm talking about the threats on Facebook. Those that you sent to C, Laura. Death threats . . . '

'What?!'

'They were sent around before you arrived. Everyone was stunned. How could you have written such things? How? Frankly, no matter what she did to you . . . I can understand that C is afraid and spoke to the police . . . I would have done the same thing . . . My God, Laura, what's happening to you? What do you want?'

She continues talking and through the buzzing in my head I can hear from a distance the same words she is repeating: 'Losing it'. 'Unthinkable'. 'Get some help'. 'Immediately'.

*

Destroy the connection between C and me. Cut it off for ever. That woman is slowly killing me. For a long time I was afraid to speak to her. I remember what Luc said—in these cases, language is of no help.

But this time it's clear I must. Act. I must act. I ring C's doorbell.

'I knew you would come.'

She has a strange smile. A manufactured lightness, but which might be considered real if one didn't know that everything about her is fake. False like the false death threats that she sent to herself from my fake Facebook account.

'You're crazy, you know.'

I'm on the threshold, and I'm shouting.

'You're sick . . . No, you realize, I hope, that you're sick . . . Really, really sick . . . that's funny?'

She maintains a disturbing calm.

'Come in,' she says. And she leads me into the kitchen with an air of saying: 'We have all the time in the world.'

' . . . '

'I'm glad you've come. We can discuss things now . . . '

I'm quiet. I wait. I'm still trying to contain myself. Explain things? Then let her start talking, good God . . . Let her talk. I can't take it any more. I'm about to scream when my eye suddenly stops at the wall. The knife collection. Her father's.

*

'Do you recognize them? He gave them to me before he died. He knew that I liked them.'

Her words are oddly detached, like on the phone.

'Knives for deboning, for cutting, for stripping, for bleeding . . . '

'Stop . . . what are you talking about?'

'The sharp edge of its blade silently slices through the meat of the muscle.'

'Stop it, do you hear me? Now I'm going to call the police. I'm going to tell them that you're dangerous. Why did you pretend that I was threatening you?'

There's something in her eyes that I haven't seen before. As sharp as her father's knives.

'Really, I just can't believe it. You made it all up, right? Then you went to find the cops and you told them that I was threatening you on Facebook? Tell me that's right. That's it, right? Right?'

Her mouth is slightly open and her lips are slowly moving . . .

'Don't you remember, Laura? In my father's butcher shop? We spent hours admiring them. The flesh, the nerves, the milky pink of the skin. Don't you remember how nice that was? But that was before. Before you *ruined everything*. Why did you destroy us? *Why*?'

She's screaming. I take a few steps back.

'We found each other again, Laura. Why didn't you ever want to admit that? Agree to love me. You preferred to destroy everything. You humiliated me. You made fun of me. How could you do such a thing?'

C is breathing heavily. She's shouting. Then her broken voice becomes silent. She looks at the wall.

'I can still hear my father . . . "Look, I scarcely move my knife and the bones separate as naturally as that . . . See how easy it is?"'

'See how easy it is?' She says in the same tone she used during the clothing scene, 'See how easy it is to be you. Easy to make you disappear.'

Then, everything is a blur. In my brain, colours—red, blood red, magenta, garnet . . . follow one another quicker and quicker, like psychedelic images. Fear. Panic. Soon a blade will strike and there will only be black.

*

Now, I'm running. Wildly. As fast as possible. Disappear into the night. In an empty cafe, I try to catch my breath. The waiter asks me if I'm OK. I can see the butterfly caught in the trap of the *Gigantiops destructor*. I wander through Paris. Until almost dawn, and I find a message from Eduardo. His voice is strange: The police came to our flat. Looking for me. C was found wounded in her kitchen.

'Bebita . . . she says that you attacked her with a knife . . . '

'No!!! . . . Eduardo . . . NO!!!!'

I'm shouting. When I open my eyes, Eduardo is bending over me. Holding my wrists. Moving them from right to left.

'Bebita . . . Hola, Bebita . . . wake up. It's nothing. Just a nightmare.'

He squeezes a bit harder. Shakes me lightly. He stays like that for a few minutes without saying anything, uneasy. Then he kisses me on the forehead . . .

'Will you be OK? Good.' He had to leave.

9

Go Away, Cry of the Living

I hear the door to the flat close. It's early, and I can still see Eduardo leaning over me. Looking at me with concern. He knows me. He knows, behind my smooth and tough exterior, just how 'delicate' I can be. 'Supercalifragilistic,' he said to me one day—I certainly didn't expect a superdisneygringolistic reference to come out of his mouth, but I loved the word spoken with his Mexican accent.

And yet, Eduardo hates it when my anxieties become too invasive. 'I've told you a hundred times, Bebita. Fear is a motor, but don't let it become . . . how do you say, dis-ab-ling . . . is that it?'

That's it. Disabling. It seems simple coming from a perfectly rational and busy businessman. But—even if I know how to let nothing slip into my work at the station—experience has proven that one can't order it. In those cases, when his humour isn't enough, Eduardo, powerless, beats a hasty retreat.

*

I don't blame him. Since he returned from Mexico, he senses that things are unsteady. He's wondering if maybe I'm losing it. If C might not be revealing a more serious problem. And he doesn't want a more serious problem. He's protecting himself. In Chiapas, when he was young, he lost his mother to a form of dementia. Which? It was difficult to know exactly. A precocious neurodegenerative illness. Eduardo doesn't talk about it much. He avoids the subject. He prefers talking about his grandmother, his Abuela. But I know he's terrified at the thought of seeing a woman he loves, and with whom he lives, sink into the depths of madness. More than anything, he fears that darkness which he cannot control.

*

bebita@gmail.com informs me that a message has just arrived. 'Hola, Bebita. Are you OK?' Eduardo must have sent this from his car. He uses phrases that have become codes between us. Magical formulas. 'We'll deal with this, you know, we've handled everything up to now. From on top . . . MUCHOS BESOS, MA BEB. See you tonight. Ed.'

*

I smile. I remember his proposition of the day before. Get a lawyer, file a complaint. However, Luc, Vincent, Riccardo and the others all told me: 'You can always tell the police about it. But it's going to be difficult. How can you describe the mortifying hold of this C? You'll have to make them understand that every word, every suggestion, every intonation, every hint is important,' Luc stressed. 'Every detail, taken separately, seems harmless. It's putting them all together that is destructive. The compulsive repetition . . . But how can you tell that to the police? "Excuse me, sir, there is a woman in my office who is obsessed with me . . . persuaded that I love her. Hostile, you see . . . " At best, they'll take you for a nut case. In any case, the police have better things to do.'

*

They were right. Eduardo would file a complaint then . . . nothing. If C were questioned she would come off beautifully. As she knows very well how to do. She would appear perfectly sane. She would say that she is being persecuted by a paranoid named Laura Wilmote. She . . . I couldn't see any possible defence. I am backed into a corner.

*

And late for work. Still shocked by my nightmare—a premonition? I had always been a bit superstitious, but I am becoming even more so, to the point of saying to myself now, like C, that everything could be 'a sign'—I quickly go down the stairs to the parking garage of our building. I am going to my car when a door slams shut behind me. Then nothing. Dead silence. I think I see C hiding behind a pillar. Hear steps, the sound of heels on the painted concrete. I have the feeling I'm in a bad horror movie. A scene in which I don't want to act. I'm terrorized.

What if . . . ? No, a door has simply shut, that's all. Now I'm having hallucinations. I, who rarely cry, burst into tears. And race back upstairs as quickly as I can.

*

As I'm going back up the stairs, out of breath, to the flat, I keep repeating: 'Stage 4. Passing to the act. She kills you or she kills herself. She kills you or . . . she kills you.'

I'm shaken by hiccups. I can't breathe. It's too much. This struggle is too much for me.

*

At that moment, I see a way out. Simple. Extreme. The only possible way. Disappear.

Leave, escape, evaporate. Some time ago Eduardo had quoted this verse from Saint-John Perse: 'Go away! Go away! Cry of the living!'

*

'To leave' suddenly becomes the most beautiful of all verbs. I roll it in my mouth, savour it like a sweet delicacy. To leave in order to start again, like a plant that grows again. To leave in order to live again. How? For how long? I don't know. After all, nothing is forcing me to leave forever. But it is now, right away, that I have to escape. Immediately, the cry of the living.

*

I like the idea of a clean break, sharp and clean. I suddenly feel incredibly light. Proud, too. Something I haven't felt for a long time. I think of de Clérambault again and of one of the last things he said when he was almost blind, feeling himself declining and having just decided to put an end to his life: 'I see light at the end of the tunnel.'

To leave, to die . . . In the country, where I grew up, people never said 'She's dead' but 'She has departed.' As if the dead were travelling, too. As if they were going somewhere.

*

With my head in my hands, at the kitchen table, I continue to gather my thoughts. Ideas keep rushing through my brain. I'm talking to myself. Softly. To try to calm the mixture of excitement and anxiety that is taking over. I had read that in a psychology magazine. Laura, Bebita, everything's going to be fine. I speak to myself as if another Me is taking care of me. And that person is so at peace, so affectionate . . . I want to be that Me. Become that Other.

*

That's how the idea crystalizes. I remember reading an article on identity theft in *Le Monde*. 'There are more and more people pretending to be someone else. According to the latest statistics, identity theft has increased by 21 per cent between 2014 and 2015.' At the beginning someone had wanted to 'be me'. Now, I am certain of it, and I would only escape by becoming someone else, in turn.

*

It happens more easily than I could have imagined. I think of Adriana, that friend of Eduardo's who in fact has just come back from Mexico. Adriana is Mexican but lives in Paris. Adriana is Mexican but anyone would think she is European. Light skin, blue eyes. Eduardo often told me that there was a certain resemblance between us. 'There was a surge in German immigration to Mexico in the nineteenth century,' he told me. 'That's when her family left Europe.'

*

Adriana has just lost her father. She went to Mexico then, but has recently returned. On the phone, I tell her it's been too long. That I would love to see her. I know that her father and she were close, in spite of the distance. I also know that he was the only family member she had left.

I go to her place, a nice little flat behind the Palais-Royal, but always a bit of a mess, with things everywhere. Adriana is a very disorganized person. This day she is sad and bedraggled.

'He was ill for a long time. But, you know, no matter how ready you are, you're never ready . . . '

'I know,' I answer, asking her where the burial took place.

She describes the ceremony, at the Santísima Trinidad, not far from Zócalo.

'That city is spreading out farther and farther, it's polluted, unlivable,' she added. 'Now that I no longer really have a reason to go there, I think I will never set foot in it again. Shall I heat some water for tea?'

*

It's then that my opportunity presents itself. Adriana goes to the kitchen to fill the kettle. At the foot of the sofa a thin, green booklet is peeking out from the jumble in her purse. *Estados Unidos Mexi* . . . I take it out with my thumb and forefinger. In a few seconds Adriana's passport has changed purses.

*

I take as few clothes as possible, as I do when I travel for an interview, my computer and a large bracelet of solid gold, a gift from my mother, easy to sell. Then I shut the door to our flat behind me. On the way to the airport, I ask the taxi driver to stop twice. At the end of the avenue du Président-Wilson I take out some money, the same amount I take out every week. Then, with the elastic band I use to tie back my hair I assemble my three credit cards, my driver's license, my chequebook, printed-out emails, photos, my press card . . . As well as my two cell phones that contain what the TV station calls 'my precious contacts' and which have taken me so many years to collect. So all that I have on me and that has my name, everything that made me me—except that I haven't been me for a long time—all of that disappears in a few seconds under the Pont de l'Alma into the flowing grey waters of the Seine.

*

Only the perilous journey is left. The final throw of the dice. I know that's what it is. Everything could blow up in a second. Luckily, Adriana's passport is an old identity document. Not biometric. That is very lucky. At the airport, the immigration officer—there are two in the glass booth—is talking politics with his colleague.

He hardly raises his eyes then quickly closes the passport on the boarding pass and hands them back to me while turning back to the other man.

*

In 1928, a young doctor joined the special infirmary of the police station. That psychiatry intern was named Jacques Lacan. De Clérambault was not impressed. He thought Lacan wasn't sincere. Lacan always respected and admired de Clérambault, the conciseness of his thinking, the perfection of his treatments. His 'clinical genius'. It was said that Lacan even borrowed his way of speaking and his overall aspect. Throughout his life Lacan described de Clérambault as 'his only professor in psychiatry'. What is surprising is that he was incapable of remembering de Clérambault's first name. He always called him Georges. Whose identity did he want de Clérambault to assume? Why did he want Gaëtan to become Georges?

*

In the aeroplane I quickly feel far away. When the stewardess comes by with the *Forma Migratoria de Turista*, I try to act nonchalant and signal no with my hand. No need. I even surprise myself. Only the thought of Eduardo, the warmth of his skin, his tenderness, still connects me to what has already become the 'world before'. Will I get used to living without him? Will I ever see him again?

*

I think of the letter I left him on the kitchen table. I asked him not to be mad at me for leaving. Without saying anything. So abruptly. I told him that I had thought of talking to him, but that exchanges—real exchanges—had become too difficult since he got back. Of course, I understood. By invading my existence C had poisoned his. But I couldn't bear also becoming slightly crazy in his eyes. C had already destroyed my professional life. It couldn't be said that she had ruined our lives, as well.

And yet, Eduardo had to understand that de Clérambault's Syndrome really did exist—it's not because one hasn't heard of an illness that it doesn't exist. And, as PH said, it can strike anyone at any time.

I attached a scientific article to the letter: 'De Clérambault's Syndrome in Sexually Experienced Women' (J. Clin. Psychiatry, 1991). Of all my documentation, this article seemed to be the clearest, the one best able to explain to the uninitiated this delusional system closed on itself, that infinite recurrence of a fixed idea, and its necessarily tragic conclusion.

The article discusses five cases of women stricken by passionate psychosis or 'love madness' (which the authors also call 'incubus syndrome'). It describes a case that had lasted thirty-seven years. Above all, the authors insist on the fact that 'since its brilliant description by the master,' the 'delusional illusion of being loved' did not involve only heterosexual women of low social status, as was thought in de Clérambault's time. Nor just women whose sexual life was non-existent or minimal. We know today that the syndrome can affect men as well as women, homosexuals and heterosexuals, and even 'people whose sex life is rich and varied, which often contradicted the chastity that was often described by de Clérambault.' Henceforth the syndrome has appeared more diffuse and all the more difficult to detect.

Could Eduardo understand that I wasn't crazy, that I didn't want to become crazy, and that, for that, I had no other escape than to disappear? Once again, I wanted the memory of our relationship not to be destroyed by this sordid affair. Because our love had always been deep, luminous and happy. Would we see each other again? I didn't know. It would depend on too many things. And I thanked him for giving me so many years of happiness and laughter.

*

Change your skin, your life, your identity, continents —was that all it took? The first days in Mexico City seemed simple and light. I found a small flat to rent in the Centro Histórico, furnished—'flooded with sunlight'—as the real-estate agent described it, an expression that I've always found just about as stupid as 'asking as a friend'. But I don't want to think about anything any more. I have cut ties one by one, even the strongest, which had connected me to Europe. I no longer read any email, I ignore the Internet, I'm not interested in the news. And I begin to enjoy the happiness of being erased from the world. Anonymous. Unreachable. Disconnected. Delivered. Distracted— but in the positive sense of the terms.

*

Gradually I rediscover sleep. Even *Gigantiops* has gone away. I feel I'm living again. With Eduardo I had often visited Chiapas, but always for short trips, brief holidays. I had never really made the effort to learn

Spanish. I was proud of that. The language barrier was a marvellous protection against reality. I was a foreigner. A piece of wood on the surface of the sea. Accepting—even savouring—the idea of not understanding everything. I developed a profound liking for these people who were so different from me and who would never have had the slightest idea of being me!

*

Anonymous in the crowd, I love wandering in the Mercado de la Merced. Colours. Smells. A frenzy of fruit. Unknown vegetables. Not far, at the Mercado de Sonora, there are all sorts of plants and grigris for witchcraft. The witch in me is never very far from my mind. But it seems that for the first time I'm managing to keep her at a distance. I've found a mastery over the situation. I am convalescing. My healing is only a matter of time . . . Avenida Fray Servando, I even buy a box of red tea with a base of damiana and vanilla bean. I don't really know what that is, but the label indicates in English that damiana was once used by the Mayans as an energizer and the vanilla beans by Aztec herbalists to sooth anxiety. After all, it couldn't do any harm. And its name is amusing: 'Anti-psychotic Blend'.

*

Maybe it is a subconscious way of thinking of Eduardo
and his grandmother's powders. To tell the truth, so
many things here make me think of him. When I think
about him my heart clenches. I miss him. But . . . how
could he not have understood anything? I immediately
ask myself. And, again, my heart clenches. Outside of
him, however, I'm not suffering from solitude at all. I
am less and less stressed. I still don't know what the
future will bring, but I am living day to day. Transformed. Unknotted. Happy?

*

One day, however, I decide to see how the TV station
has 'handled' my disappearance. The show can still be
downloaded on the website. After the generic sound-
track, the first image I see makes me freeze. C is there,
smiling and perfectly made up—the same red lipstick
that I kept in my drawer with my dance shoes. C is
there on my set, seated in my club chair, opposite the
historian Laurent Golding and the psychoanalyst
Muriel Trevor. With the greatest of ease she then turns
to Valérie Trierweiler.

'Madame Trierweiler, you have often been presented as . . . don't you think that jealousy . . . '

I can't listen to any more. I move the cursor to the end of the show. But, when I pick up my finger an even more gripping spectacle is awaiting me. 'This is the forty-third day since the disappearance of our colleague Laura Wilmote,' says C, solemnly showing a black-and-white photo of me to the camera. 'Laura, if you're alive, and I'm sure that you are . . . Laura, if you hear this message, come back. Answer, Laura. We'll take care of you.'

*

That isn't all. A bit later, on the site of a major newspaper, I discover a long article signed by C. I have the feeling I'm reading my own obituary. C isn't giving me up for dead, not obviously, but she entitled her piece ambiguously on my 'disappearance'. Between the lines one could read that after the police inquiry, which led to no serious information, the worst is now to be feared.

'The abrupt disappearance of Laura Wilmote has affected far more than media professionals,' she wrote. 'A number of people from the world of culture have spoken of a rigorous and demanding journalist and have expressed their sadness in the face of this unexplained disappearance.

'The former ENS student with a masters in philosophy, Laura Wilmote had given up an academic career to devote herself to her passions, journalism and writing. After having worked in the print media, she joined television where she spent most of her career. First in the cultural realm, then as a reporter, before hosting the themed programme that made her famous.

'Famous is perhaps not the right word. Laura Wilmote didn't trust fame. Like all great journalists she wasn't blanketed in certainty. She doubted, scrupulously sought out the sources of her information, meticulously analysed those sources. It was probably doubt that led her to empathize with those she interviewed. And which explains those exquisite portraits she did of personalities in the world of art, science and culture.

'For her TV programme, she always chose her guests with the greatest care, prepared each of her shows with them, and, a diligent worker, a perfectionist, mastered each of her subjects in the tiniest detail.

'Doubt as the salt of the mind, but also as an invisible defect . . . Her professional entourage describes her as "passionate and fragile". Recently, her behaviour had become strange, aggressive. At the station one of her colleagues, who prefers to remain anonymous, was heard to say that a serious "romantic disappointment" could be at the origin of her disappearance. In her last novel, Laura Wilmote had in fact chosen to explore the theme of impossible love.

'Reactions to the announcement of her disappearance have been overwhelmingly emotional, reflecting the esteem in which she was held by the worlds of culture and journalism. Her ideas, her charm, her talent continue to guide us. I dare to believe that she would say that that is all that counts.'

*

'All that counts?' That bitch . . . I close the page by furiously clicking on the little X on the upper right. 'Anonymous colleague!' 'Aggressive behaviour!' 'Serious romantic disappointment!' those lies knock around in my head. 'You lose nothing by waiting,' I tell myself. I smile while thinking of Mark Twain: 'The reports of my death are greatly exaggerated.'

*

In 1934 de Clérambault was sixty-two. His sight continued to deteriorate. The fear of becoming blind made him neurasthenic. Arthritis affected his back constantly. Nevertheless, he made it a point of honour to continue to direct his service. He continued to present his patients. At the end of the year, however, everything became too difficult for the head doctor of the special infirmary. In November, in the beautiful house in which he lived at 46 rue Danicourt, in Malakoff, he composed his last will. A bachelor, he bequeathed his entire estate to charity. He wished that his ethnographic slides be placed in the Trocadéro museum— he was always enthralled with the art of drapery and took thousands of photos of tunics, cloth, costumes in Morocco . . . Then he did an accounting of his food: '4.90 F for a lobster, and 1.25 F for a bottle of cognac,' notes his biographer. Who adds: 'The attention paid to little things in life by a melancholic in the imminence of a violent death will always be a mystery.' Ultimately, he took his service revolver, went up to his attic, and, in front of a large armoire made of glass and acajou, put the gun in his mouth and pulled the trigger.

*

Today, in my tiny kitchen in the Centro Histórico, I feel a desperate hatred overtake me. Like de Clérambault, I feel the need for a definitive ending. An act that would be as sharp as a gun shot. A liberating detonation.

*

When I left for Mexico it seemed—and I am proud of this—that I had escaped the alternative: 'She'll kill herself or kill you.' I thought I had found a third route. Now everything is falling apart. My strategy of reconquest. My almost rediscovered serenity. But now C is catching me again. Even here. Has she really won?

*

Death. Give it or give it to oneself. The only outcome. The final step. I understand de Clérambault. He and I—I have now spent so much time in his thoughts and in his books that I can allow myself that slightly pretentious familiarity—he and I, then, have things in common. We have confronted that fearsome category of insanity—'reasoning madmen'. Those who speak, write, discuss and argue so artfully that everyone thinks they're normal. Those who carry on masked or so well covered that they have that horrible ability to blend into the masses. And to turn around every situation—the sick one is always you. Reasoning madmen, I say to myself, the worst . . . And then, something profound links me to de Clérambault. We are both proud and 'fragile'. I can understand what he did only too well. He hadn't accepted to decline, through his own eyes or in those of others. He was enwrapped —this describes de Clérambault—in his pride and his

141

dignity. As for me, I had left because C was rotting me from the inside. But also because I could no longer bear the looks of those around me. Incredulous. Suspicious. That Eduardo, my mother, my colleagues . . . would consider me crazy—and that perhaps they were right.

*

Is madness contagious? The press of the time said that 'a half-mad was directing the mad'. 'An existence spent amidst the mad, maniacs, great neurotics, and delusional people perhaps played a part in provoking certain bizarre character traits in Doctor de Clérambault,' one reads in the *Aliéniste français*. The bizarre behaviour? De Clérambault himself was an obsessive. For example, the Moroccan cloths of which he took more than 5,000 photos. Always different, always the same. His biographer notes that 'he lived with the crazy ambition of mounting a global cartography of cloths, from the study of Arab costumes to that of the clothing of American Indians.'

*

Was de Clérambault half-crazy? He was obsessive, in any case. In his own way. A character trait to which could be added his misogyny and his anti-Semitism—both certainly typical of his time, but always disturbing when they appeared in his writings—and all that perhaps flowed from his familial genealogy or his position at the special infirmary, coldness, loftiness, scorn. Or what people took as that. For, I tell myself—and this contributed to my connection with him—between scorn and misunderstanding, there is only one step. Perhaps that of envy?

*

After de Clérambault's death, the writer Joseph Kessel was one of the only people to immediately grasp the importance of his work. His role as head of the school in contemporary psychiatry and his efforts to scientifically connect it to neurology. In *Le Figaro* of 4 December 1934, he relates a conversation he overheard between some doctors: 'Yes,' said one of them. 'There can be no doubt. Our age will have counted two men of genius in this realm. On one end, Freud. On the other, the combatant with equal power, with as much intelligence, verve and intensity, Gaëtan Gatian de Clérambault.'

10

A Punishment from Elsewhere

And I thought that Mexico was going to slowly heal the wounds. But the pain and anger have returned. And they persist, as strong as ever. C had succeeded in taking everything from me, the station, my work, my show, Eduardo, my country, my passport and even my name. She had possessed me, and dispossessed me. And, as if that weren't enough, she also left me for dead in the press. The abrupt disappearance of Laura Wilmote . . . that was the last straw. I imagine Eduardo parodying his favourite hero, Edmond Dantès, with his inimitable accent: 'I vill haf my reevenge!'

*

Eduardo had told me that Dumas's hero was inspired by the true story of someone called François Picaud. 'You see,' he told me, while we were discussing the difference between avengers and justices, 'Picaud never could have been the hero of a novel. He, himself, killed those who had robbed him and stolen his fiancée. But he eliminated them savagely. Without mercy. Whereas Dantès goes about things differently. Mondego kills himself, Danglars is ruined, Villefort wallows in dementia. Everything happens as if a hand from an unknown place has taken charge of the punishment. Isn't that absolutely beautiful?'

*

I dream of a vengeance like Dantès'. A punishment that comes from somewhere else. A murder without a murderer. Do I need to kill her? Could I just be happy frightening her?

I think about it. C has taken everything from me. The only thing I brought with me was the intimate knowledge of her madness. A profound understanding of de Clérambault's Syndrome, its stages, its mechanisms.

*

A scene with PH keeps coming back to me. 'What would happen,' I asked him one day, 'if I said to C, in the end, why not? That I agreed . . . after all, the fact that I was repelling her advances most probably heightened her desire. What if I followed her lead? If I told her yes?' I had suggested to PH with a certain bravado. From that point of view, at least the de Clérambault patient is like everyone else, right? Doesn't she get tired once her desire is satisfied?

'Like everyone else?' replied PH, astonished. Then, convinced that I was joking, he burst out laughing. 'Right . . . get closer . . . go ahead . . . Really, Laura, such craziness wouldn't occur to anyone. Except, perhaps, a novelist lost in the labyrinth of her stories.'

*

Later, nonchalantly, I asked the question again. Regarding Johnny and his stalker.

'She would kill him, I think . . . "You understand, Doctor . . . Someone pretending to be Johnny wanted . . . So I had to kill him."'

PH had rubbed his moustache, looked off in the distance. Then he concluded, 'A hetero-aggressive attack or suicide—she would kill him or kill herself. There is no curing erotomaniacs. No solution to their delusion.'

*

No solution? I see one, on the contrary. I had finally managed, not without some difficulty, to close the fake Facebook page. Today I recreate one. In the same name. The simplest—my own, Laura Wilmote. Suddenly I become myself again. I exist once again. I begin writing to her.

*

'C? It's me, Laura . . . '

*

As expected, I don't receive a response. I continue: 'C, are you there? It's Laura. Tell me you're getting these messages . . . '

*

'I need to contact you. It's urgent.'

*

Now, I'm the one bombarding her with messages.

*

'Dear C,

You're not answering me. But I'll continue to write to you. What I want to tell you is very important.

First, I owe you an explanation. I know now that you were right. All along you were able to see clearly inside me. Whereas I, pardon me, I was in the darkness.'

*

I let some time go by. I go to fix a cup of 'Anti-Psychotic Blend'. Then I sit back down at my computer and continue my surrealist monologue.

*

'Blinded by fear. That idiotic fear of conventions. Buried by the confusion of my feelings, I made you suffer, C. I made you suffer wrongly. You who only wanted what was best for me. For us.'

*

Still no answer. But I am confident in my strategy. The image in my mind is that of a tug-of-war game. Each person pulls on his end with all his strength, but the strengths cancel each other out. It's only when one person stops pulling—or moves in the direction of the other—that the other falls. I continue:

'Everything seems so clear now. I needed some time, you're in a good position to know that. It took me some time, yes, but you have opened my eyes.'

*

On the fourth day, C, who usually responded immediately, has still not appeared. I continue:

'That happiness that is there, within arm's length, we're going to experience it for ever. Believe me, my C.'

C takes five days to send three words: 'Who are you?'

*

I write more and more:

'My dear C,

Tell me you're not angry at me . . . Every day I regret my behaviour. My stinginess. My stubbornness. I was a caged bird. Caught in the cage of mores and codes. While you were telling me the truth: I love you.'

*

'Now it's as clear as the clearest water. What could be clearer or more beautiful? Or more joyful? Yes, my C, I've finally understood. I'm opening my arms. I'm here. I love you.'

*

Again, those three words: 'Who are you?'

*

'My very dear C,

I'm thinking of you. Of your slender legs, your elegant shoes. Your neck and its beautiful, smooth, pale skin. I see the reflections of your silk blouse, like mine, unbuttoned. You were right. We are unique. You and I are but One.

Your Laura.'

*

Message from C:

'You're not Laura. You're lying. Tell me who you are and what you want.'

*

'My C,

It's me, don't be afraid. I'm Laura, YOUR Laura. Why has it come to this, my C? Why did we ever separate?'

*

'My C,

I need you. Are you really that angry with me? Have your feelings for me changed? Do I no longer inhabit your thoughts the way you are, endlessly, wrapped up in mine?'

*

Message from C:

'I KNOW that you're not her. You're pretending to be her because you want to dirty our story. If you're Laura, why did you leave?'

*

'I left, but I'm coming back. Here I am, C. You can be sure . . .'

*

Message from C:

'You've invented this imposture from the start. To play with my feelings and my suffering. Who are you?'

*

'My C,

Don't be afraid. Me, too, now, I will always be there for you.'

*

I continue like that. Intimacy and warmth ramping up. I write faster and faster. A flood of words. While I'm typing my determination increases. I can see C's face on the screen, instead of mine, on my show. Her idiocies in front of my guests. Her falsity. I hear her presumably humanitarian and perfectly Machiavellian appeal: 'Laura, if you hear me, come back.' I tell myself that I am fulfilling her wish. I am returning. I am a ghost playing *her* scenario in reverse. Perfect symmetry— now it is I who am sending her messages at the moment she least expects them. She who is feeling attacked, stalked. And I who am telling her not to be afraid. Using her words, her expressions, her 'methods'.

*

'No solution to the delusion' . . . But what if the delusion became the solution? The means to tear apart the web she had caught me in? I have to bring her to the heart of her syndrome, push her to the depths, force her into it. We have to reach that point of no return that PH described. 'You understand, Doctor . . . '

*

I continue my messages, increasing the tempo.

'My very dear C,

I think so often of that moment that clicked in you. Not the one that made you aware that you loved me. That would have been too banal. No, the one that made you understand that I loved YOU . . . '

*

'My C,

That you had that revelation, that you were able to persist in your certainty when I was so resistant, increases my admiration for you. What clarity. What determination. You could have lowered your arms a thousand times, my C. How lucky I've been . . . Thanks to you, to that incredible clairvoyance, but also to your tenacity and courage, our love can be expressed. Tell me that you still want it, my C. Tell me. I need to hear it . . . '

*

At the beginning I felt a strange sensation in sending C love messages. But quickly that feeling dissipated. The words continue to flow out of me almost automatically. The important thing is that she receive more and more of them. And faster and faster. That she feel besieged. 'Either she kills you, or she kills herself.' C had a gun in mind. I had to get her to turn it around. To turn that gun on herself.

*

And so I send even more messages, even faster. Then I send these lines:

'My C,

I need to see you now. We're going to see each other. You will take me in your arms. I will feel your breath on my hair. I will be wrapped in you, and you in me. And, as you so often told me, we will be but one . . .

Listen, my C. Let's meet at the Hotel Molitor. You know, the place where the Press Club cocktail party was, near the Auteuil gardens. We'll be alone for our reunion. I'll wait for you there Friday at 7 p.m. I can't wait.

Your Laura.'

11

Seeing the Other as He Isn't

I admit I'm not unhappy. To pretend to be who one truly is—isn't that what Eduardo would call absolute perfection?

*

Eduardo . . . I hear myself sigh . . . I would give anything to feel his arms around me. I would really like for him to be in my place. For him to make this effort. For him to understand me. What has happened since I disappeared? How has he reacted? What psychological state must he be in? For several days I've been asking myself those questions. I come up with hypotheses. What about the police investigation? Did Adriana end up discovering her passport was gone? Did she file a complaint? Some days I tell myself that that is what I would have done. And then I would immediately see myself in her situation. Since I travelled a lot for my work I often lost or misplaced my passport. Did I put it away when I got off the aeroplane? It's never in the right purse. Never in the desk drawer. I never worried about it too much. 'Eduardo, did you happen to see my p...?' He rolled his eyes. He knew as well as I did that I always ended up finding it. In any case, it would have never occurred to me to think someone had taken it...

*

I also wonder—a bizarre idea—if they put up fliers at the Paris airport. I don't know why, but I'm always fascinated by the photos of missing persons in airports. Laura Wilmote: 'Fair skin, blue eyes.' 'Disappeared in Paris.' 'Vermist in Paris.' 'desaparecida en Paris.' 'Sparita a Parigi'...

*

Mainly, I'm worried for Eduardo. What is he thinking? About me? About us? About all of this? Maybe it's my propensity for feeling guilty, but negative ideas keep surging up. Was I right to chalk up his distance to his lack of time? Wasn't that an excuse that I made up for myself? And his mother's illness? The fact that he was so reluctant to approach that of C. Was it really because the irrational brought up too many bad memories in him? After all, I was the one who told those stories.

Through professional deformation? Because I couldn't help myself from making up stories among which I would choose those that suited me best? Eduardo always got out of our conversations through pirouettes. Making me laugh was his favourite sport. Connected with the need to be the strongest—'I am the one in your life, Bebita, who has made you laugh the most, isn't that right, Beb?' Then he would conclude, 'We have a lot of fun together, don't we?' And those words would always make me think of the ones that Romain Gary left on his deathbed just before he killed himself: 'I had a lot of fun.'

*

Yes, Eduardo made me laugh. But what did he really think, deep down? Recently it seemed that I saw clouds of doubt pass over his face. Could he wonder whether all of this was my fault? Because I wanted to write the damned novel? Eduardo has always known that I'm a flirt, that I like being pursued. Maybe he was telling himself that I fanned C's flame on purpose? To be the centre of her attention? To hold power over her and enjoy doing it? Did he wonder if I was attracted to C?

*

Were my supercalifragilities beginning to tire him? Did he love me less?

*

In the end, the temptation is too great. I open bebita@gmail.com:

'You have 47 unread messages.'

*

'Bebita, your two cell phones are ringing in the void. I've left you thousands of messages. We need to talk, Bebita. Call me. Soon.'

*

'Bebita, it is incredibly late. I can't sleep. "No other choice but to disappear." I hope you weren't serious. Call me, POR FAVOR.'

*

'Where are you in the middle of the night, my Beb????
Have you run away? But your car is in the courtyard.
I'm worried. LLAMAME POR FAVOR. AHORITA.'

*

'Bebita, I haven't slept a wink. I keep thinking of our
conversation. This morning I spoke with my lawyer.
Call me.'

*

'Why aren't you calling? Please, at least tell me you're
OK.'

*

'Bebita, are you angry with me? Give me a sign, I beg
you. Just to tell me you're OK.'

*

'I'm sad, Bebita. Have you given me up? Did you leave
with a lover? Why won't you answer me???? Do you
want me to leave you alone? I've probably not been

attentive enough, but you're abandoning me like that. Without hesitation.'

*

'Bebita, I'm not asking where you are. I just want to know you're OK, because I'm worried. Your brothers, your sisters and your mother are worried, too. I was hoping you had gone to stay with one of them. I called the station. You hadn't contacted them, either. You're not on assignment. No one can understand.'

*

'The police tell me to wait a few days. "People who disappear, we find them, if I may say so, sir, sorry, it's an expression, out the wazoo. You know how many . . . etc." I'm telling you, to wait without news is torture every minute, Bebita. Call—I'm begging you. Or answer this email.'

*

'Bebita, the days go by, the police investigation is leading nowhere. Where are you?'

*

'They've finally decided to bring in Interpol. I don't know where you are, but I'm sure you're alive.'

*

'Another thing I'm sure of—I should have begun with this—is that your C is indeed crazy. A dangerous nut case, you were right. I know, it's a little late to have realized it. You tried to tell me ever since I returned from Mexico and I didn't listen to you. But here's what happened. You had barely left when she started inundating me with messages and emails—don't ask me how she got my contact info. Maybe you gave them to the HR department at the station? She's convinced that I know where you are. My mailbox is overflowing, my answering machine is going to explode. C says one thing over and over: she knows that I know . . .

If you've run away, it's so you won't have any news of her, I'm aware of that. Just know that, in the past few days, she's in front of our door every night. She threw herself at me yesterday, screaming, claiming that I was hiding you, that I was a bastard, that she was going to turn me in. How could I have put you through such misery?'

*

'The scene repeated itself today, except that she went farther. She said . . . well, everything you told me. That you were in love with her without admitting it to yourself, but that you had managed to let her know that. That you were unhappy but that she was going to save you. Yes, she was, not me. I'm the one who was preventing you from going to meet her whereas, most certainly, at that moment, you had understood your destiny. She articulated these words slowly and bizarrely, my Beb. "This is her destiny." And she kept repeating that happiness was within your reach. Before I locked you up, that is . . . I couldn't listen to any more. When I called the cops she left, but I saw her walking around outside. I admit she frightened me.'

*

'Today, she made an appeal on the TV: "Laura, if you're alive, return . . . " She has taken your place. In your chair. I had goose bumps.'

*

'I'm stopping here, Bebita. I just wanted to tell you that I saw the (well) hidden face of this C. Why just now? I guess I had to wait to be stalked, myself, to understand. You must find that horrible. But if I'm telling you this it is also to tell you that there is a certainty that I share with her—you're alive. That's why I'm writing to you every day, my Beb. If you're reading these messages, as I hope you are, you must feel that I'm with you.'

*

'I'm writing to you a bit like Scheherazade told his stories. To keep the Prince awake and to save his skin. I'm writing this journal of absence so that my Absent One will read it and, who knows, perhaps she'll manage to smile a bit—even if I'm aware that I'm not very funny right now . . . In any case, you're not alone, my Beb. I'm here. I love you.'

*

'I'm trying to make amends—is that how you say it? Why "amends", anyhow? Can you explain it? Anyway, I don't understand anything. I ignored what you were trying to tell me. I chalked it up to your fragilities, it was easier. Cowardly, no doubt . . . In any case, it's to repair this "defect of words"—the fact that you were unable either to talk to me, or to feel listened to—that

I've decided to write to you, begging each day for a response. I know, that doesn't change anything. I woke up too late, the harm is done. Whatever happens, you are in each of my thoughts. I want to see you again, Bebita. That's all that matters. Tell you that I understand, beg your forgiveness. I was going to write that this single thought obsesses me, but I know that under the circumstances that verb is not a great choice . . .

'But it's my turn to be obsessed. Obsessed by obsession. Thanks to you, I've even read de Clérambault's books! Not only those that I found in your office, or articles you refer to in your letter—how many times have I read and reread that letter. But other books that I had my secretary get for me. I found works that you don't seem to have had—not easy, since his works are not easy to find. And I learnt a great deal— you'd be proud of your Ed!'

*

'Did you know that Lacan considered de Clérambault his absolute master? And that, when he died, I can't remember which writer, I think it was Kessel—for whom, as you know, I have a weakness because of his *The Passerby*—well, Kessel is believed to have said that de Clérambault was as intelligent as Freud. I also came upon that story of the French neurologist Gilles de la

Tourette. In 1893, a woman—I'm guessing it was one of his patients—came to wait for him at his home. When he met her in his office, she shot him with a revolver, shouting, "You love me, I'm killing you." I found a drawing of that scene in a magazine. I've attached it so you can have a laugh. Look at the hat and gloves the murderess is wearing—total Belle Époque! (but be sure to check that it's really a matter of eroto-mania before you use it in your book).'

*

'This evening, my Beb, I'm really low. I shouldn't tell you that, I know. I'm your *hombre más fuerte de México*. Do you remember at San Luis Potisí? We came upon that hilarious competition to choose *los hombres más Fuertes de la Republica Mexicana*? "Con la presencia de competidores de todos los estados," yelled the guy into the microphone. The ladies were in a frenzy. Cameras danced around those huge hunks in "Strongman" tees who were picking up cars, boulders, weights in the shapes of skulls. You chose me to be *más fuerte para hacer reír toda América del Sur*. Tonight, my Beb, your strongman is deathly afraid.'

*

'I shouldn't tell you this, either. Do you know what really hurts me, deep down? The idea that "we" didn't count. That you were obsessed with this thing and that our relationship was only second. That you could leave me like that. For a reason that had nothing to do with us. It really hurts. You didn't trust me, my Beb. You decided to leave, and nothing could stop you. You must have thought, "He's going to betray me, betray my secret." You treated me like everyone else. All the others. And I thought I was loved . . . Was that an illusion?'

*

'I'm sorry, my Beb. But it's been forty-seven days now that everyone has been looking for you. I admit that there are moments when I lose heart.'

*

'The good news is that the river brigade hasn't found anything. No "floater", as they say. The other day, I rode with them in their boat. Parkas, hoods and life jackets, there are even women in this unit, did you know? They let me in the boat, they must have seen how upset I was. Suicide attempts (they call them SA), there are around a hundred a year in the Seine. But I refuse to believe it. Where are you hiding, by Beb? Even if you never want to speak to me again, at least let me know you're OK, ¿DE ACUERDO?'

*

'The police think you haven't left Europe. Perhaps that you're not even that far away. I suddenly remembered what you told me one day. About that place where you once stayed as a writer in residence. The Chartreuse de Neuville. "A perfect place for disappearing." That hit me. I took your little black car, Black Beauty, and drove there. On the way I remembered what you told me— you see, I did listen to you, my Beb. When Hugo had made Jean Valjean disappear, he chose this place. La Madelaine-sous-Montreuil. Valjean hid there under the name of M. Madeleine. Was I going to find my Laura Wilmote under the improbable pseudonym of Mme Neuville?'

*

'When I got there I immediately understood what you meant. Lots of huge buildings, rows of vaulted edifices as far as the eye could see, cloisters, houses of the priests with their little gardens all together . . . All of that open to the world, empty, far from everything. A decommissioned quasi-city, but still functioning on its own. Protected from the world by enormous walls. A wonderful place, indeed, to escape from the world.'

*

'When I had finished looking around it, the sun was setting, the crows were shouting full force. But my strong intuition had ended up at nothing. You weren't there. I was going to leave, shattered, when I noticed a woman "of a certain age" who was returning from the garden with some vegetables. I spoke to her about you. Laura Wilmote, yes, she remembered very well. She was a volunteer who took care of the writers in residence—those contemplatives who came from time to time to stay at the monastery and for whom they had renovated part of a wing.'

*

'No, she hadn't seen you, but she remembered. "Look, that was her room . . . " She proposed that I stay the night in that room . . . By the way, I don't know how you managed to stay so long in that place, my Beb. I know you're not afraid of solitude or silence. That you have a weakness for old, unused places, but . . . such a life of an Anchorite—I've just learnt that word, you see . . .

'In fact, I'm writing this evening from your monastery, staying in your former nun's cell . . . And I'm reading . . . what do you think? De Clérambault!

'P.S. 1. There is a pile of empty jars of fluoxetine in a corner of the metal cupboard painted apple green.

'P.S. 2. I read on Google: "Fluoxetine is used to treat depression or OCD (obsessive-compulsive disorder) in adults. Also known by the trade name Prozac." It wasn't you who were taking that stuff, I hope?'

*

'Bebita,

'It's night, and I'm still reading de Clérambault. You're going to say that it's a bit late, that I'm repeating myself, but like you I find this syndrome amazing. Such stuff of fiction, in fact—except that now I'm wary of novels . . . The next time, please, choose to write short stories. And on more pleasant subjects than psychiatric pathologies ☺.'

*

'That Léa who chained herself to the gates of Buckingham Palace first made me think of the environmentalist Zadists today, chained to trees or tractors. ZAD for Zone of Abnormal Delusion. That describes C's brain pretty well, don't you think?'

*

'Listen, Bebita. Léa talks about the persecutions she endured: "People followed her, people have 'the mania of signs'; they also make noises in their throats and above all sniffling, so that their association is called 'The Snot'." And what about Léa? She is in a "flying prison, a moving cage, perpetual chains". The world upside down. Going where?'

*

'I've read about many cases of delusional illusions of being loved. For example, that of Leontine who claimed that the captain she's in love with is not married. A bit as if C insisted that you and I never lived together!! That's really it, anyway . . . I've come to understand that, in C's mind, I never existed. De Clérambault insisted. For the Subject, the Object is free. His marriage isn't valid. And the Object can have no happiness without him, the Subject, the suitor (that is, C). In other words, when C claims that I am hiding you, she believes that's the truth in every meaning of the term. The fact that we're together "isn't valid". It is an artificial link that prevents you from being happy. In sum, I'm a sadist. A pervert. I keep you tied to me to better torment and destroy you.'

*

'I can also see that most of the cases described by de Clérambault ended with: a "chronic, dangerous patient. Tenacious and impulsive, will certainly end up trying to kill the Object or him/herself." I remember your nightmare. Was that it, Bebita? That was it, wasn't it?'

*

'It is very late. The reflections of the moon stick strangely on all the iron crosses standing up around this monastery. I can see them from the window of your nun's cell and my thoughts are drifting. That must be the effect of my reading—I suddenly see de Clérambault's Syndrome everywhere. The people here have stuck religious texts on the wall, lyrics to songs or who knows what . . . God loves me . . . A great love is waiting for me . . .

I suddenly tell myself that this certainty that believers have that someone loves them, someone they've never seen, an abstraction that they themselves have created . . . the fact that this certainty, as massive and solid as the stones of this place, directs their entire life . . . don't you think that resembles a vast 'delusional illusion of being loved?' A giant de Clérambault's Syndrome that has lasted centuries and which would have led you, you Europeans, to deny, to harass, to torture, to burn alive—notably in my country, Mexico—and in the name of what, if not a 'prideful construction of your imagination'? A collective construction that has become dominant to such a degree that no one, even today, is surprised any more . . . '

*

'You'll tell me it's late, that I'm wandering. You're right. I just wonder if there isn't a slightly amusing parallel to be made, in your crazy novel, between the passionate delusions and the mass psychoses which religions make me think of when they show us what is worst about them. But after all, you're the Brainiac. Maybe you've already thought of that . . . ?'

*

'Obviously, I haven't told the woman anything about all this. The next day, delightful, she prepared breakfast for me with toast and honey made on site. She wanted to show me the monks' garden, the seeds she harvested, the "simple" ones—can you explain why they're simple? Are there "complicated" plants? My thoughts were elsewhere, I was disoriented. Usually, I wouldn't have spent the time on such a visit. But then I imagined you in the garden paths. I told myself that you must have liked it, wrote down the names of these plants I had never heard of—giant hyssop, skullcap, coltsfoot, saponaria, burnet, lemon balm, and catmints, bear's garlic, hellebore . . . '

*

'In front of the hellebore, in fact, the lady stopped. She remembered that you were interested in botany. You had spoken together of hellebore which "purged the most tenacious black bile and the dark humours . . . "

'"At least, that's what the ancient Greeks thought, you know, that it cured madness . . . We discussed that with your . . . with Laura. I noted that she knew a lot about melancholia throughout the ages."'

*

'She said that while pulling out a weed. When she stood up she turned to me. "Perhaps I shouldn't tell you but . . . Your wife, well, Laura . . . She was, how can I put it . . . vulnerable. Very vulnerable, in fact. She must have doubted her own balance. In any case, she doubted herself. Unhealthily so. She said she was stupid, that she would never amount to anything. That she battled with language. Including in her books. It gave her the impression of being locked up inside herself. An inner cage . . . Maybe that's why . . . What? She never told you any of this? . . . What happened during her stay?"

'I shook my head, no.

"One day, she was found unconscious."'

*

'An overdose. Five days in the hospital. Why didn't you ever tell me, my Laura? Why?'

*

'On the way back to Paris I was completely stunned. How could you have been so misleading! INCLUDING

TO ME? I thought again of C. You told me you were wrong about her. That you thought she was your friend and that, when you saw her true face, you felt horribly hurt. But you had insisted on something else—even more than her madness, what haunted you and which you couldn't forgive yourself for, was to have fallen into the trap. Had I, too, been taken in by you? Like all those who saw you as the strong and ambitious woman that you always seemed to be? To see the Other as she isn't—is that how it is for us all?'

*

'In Paris, my cell phone rang. I really hoped it was you. Unfortunately, once again, it was C. I was so disoriented that I picked it up. A flood of words . . . And, again, I didn't understand at all. She KNEW, she kept saying. She knew that it was me. I was the impostor who had sent those messages pretending to be Laura. It could only be me. I was shocked. What did she mean, messages? I didn't understand anything but I didn't say a word. So she would keep talking as long as possible. I hoped that, in her ranting, I would learn where you are.

'In fact, my silence only made her madder. Her words became increasingly incoherent and furious, they were those of a profoundly disturbed person.

Capable of anything. She was coming tomorrow, she ended by saying. If I thought she was going to lie down in front of a bastard like me. She was sure that I was hiding you and that I had planned this strategy to get rid of her. So she was coming. She would be there, at the Molitor, at 7 p.m. to kill me.'

*

'Bebita, I don't know anything about this meeting tomorrow, but my lawyer advises me to go under police protection. I recorded her call. We now have a death threat, you understand? I hope she'll be armed. There will be two policemen with me.'

Epilogue

Friday, 23 June, it's in the 90s in Mexico City. I look at the weather in Paris: 'Dry, sunny, with a chance of thunderstorms later in the day.' I go through my suitcase looking for the cell phone I bought in the Paris airport and never used. At the corner of Calle Venustiano Carranza, I buy a prepaid calling card. Then I try to remember the layout of the Molitor, the shape of the terrace, the dangerous area.

*

At 5.00 Paris time, I send the first text: 'My C, I can't wait for 7.' At 6 I write: 'Only another hour.'

*

I imagine her, the past few nights, waking up in a sweat, soaking wet, haggard. Tossing and turning, unable to go back to sleep. Wondering about my messages. Refusing to believe that I am the sender, but also not being able to be certain that it isn't me. Then understanding—the impostor was Eduardo.

*

'An impostor . . . Do you understand, Doctor. AND SO I HAD TO . . . ' I imagine her ready for anything. Whipped into an emotional frenzy.

*

At 6.50 I write: 'I've just arrived, my C. I'm waiting for you patiently and impatiently.'

7.00, C: 'Where are you?'

7.00, I: 'On the terrace, as we said.'

7.01, C: 'I don't see you.'

7.02: 'The small terrace, behind the bar.'

7.04, C: 'Where? I don't see you.'

7.05, C: 'Hey, are you going to tell me where you are?'

7.05, C: 'You're playing with me!'

7.06, I: 'Playing with you? Wait, I'll call you. It will be easier.'

*

'We're going to start over at the beginning, my C. I want to tell you that I thought about you at the Café des Arts and that I was touched at the idea that you went looking for me so far. I want us to return to the conversation we had at the Trocadéro cafe. Tell me about that look the night of my book signing. I'm not playing with you. I want to begin everything over, you understand?'

*

Silence. I think of the pending storm. Has it come? I imagine a bolt of lightning in the distance. Eduardo and his two cops ready to pounce.

'Laura? Is it possible? Laura, it's really you . . . You're lying . . . '

There's something strangled in her voice. An insurmountable dilemma . . .

I hear a shout. 'Ed . . . ' then I don't hear anything.

*

I wonder what the sound of a body that . . .

I imagine the rubbernecks standing there, the lights flashing, the ambulance . . .

A yellow-and-black strip. A security perimeter.

From that height . . . Only a couple seconds . . . No time to feel pain . . .

*

I am still listening. The cell phone is picking up strange sounds. At one point I hear Eduardo's voice.

*

Later, this story on the Internet:

www.afp./comfr/societe/faitdivers—Friday, 23 June at 7.13 p.m., a woman fell from the roof terrace of the Hotel Molitor on rue Nungesser-et-Coli, near the Bois de Boulogne in Paris. The investigation will determine whether it was an accident, a suicide or murder.

Acknowledgements

I've always been interested in the connections between literature, neuroscience and psychoanalysis. I first heard about Gaëtan Gatian de Clérambault from Martin Hirsch, before I encountered him again in the novel by Ian McEwan, *Enduring Love* (Jonathan Cape, 1997). For an excellent look at the life of this great alienist, I strongly recommend the biography by Alain Rubens, *Le Maître des insensés* (Les Empêcheurs de penser en rond, 1998). In addition, many doctors, psychiatrists, neurologists and scientists helped me in my research: Lucian Chasteller David Cohen, Jean-Yves Edel, Jean Garrabé, Marion Leboyer, Luc Mallet, Salah El Mestikawy, Pietro Musillo, Elena Pasquinelli, Pierre Planat as well as Dr Raphaëlle Hirsch, who kept me on the edge of my seat with the stories of her internship in psychiatry. I'd like to thank everyone, as well as Mathilde Hirsch and Betty Noiville, whose advice was extremely helpful, Juliette Hirsch, my Facebook advisor, and Stéphanie Polack for a conversation at Brasserie Balzar in Paris. And I would like especially to thank Alexia (whose name was changed) and her parents, as well as the psychoanalyst Pierre-Henri Castel and the philosopher Marc Crépon, for their help and great friendship.

This novel was completed at the Chartreuse de Neuville in Pas-de-Calais. I thank the entire team who welcomed me there. First a monastery, the Chartreuse then became a psychiatric hospital and is now a place for writers in residence. The monk, the mad, the writer—perhaps they are all a bit the same . . .